GABE'S OBSESSION

Purgatory Masters Duet

E.M. GAYLE

Gypsy Ink Books

GABE'S OBSESSION

Purgatory Masters Duet

Purgatory Masters Series

Copyright © 2017 E.M. Gayle

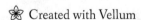 Created with Vellum

PURGATORY MASTERS DUET

GABE'S OBSESSION

GABE'S RECKONING

Gabe's Obsession, Purgatory Masters Book 4

She needs to remember the past and he knows just the thing to help her.

The moment her brother told her she killed their father, Nina couldn't breathe. The second Gabe looked at her unsure she wanted to die.

Nina had always known a chunk of her life was missing, now she knows why. Her brothers have been keeping her secrets for more than a decade.

And Gabe, the man she's WANTED for as long as she can remember, demands answers she doesn't have. The kind of answers once known will never be forgotten or forgiven.

Gabe has waited a long time for Nina to come around. Her disdain for his lifestyle seemed like a barrier between them that couldn't be broken.

Until secrets more explosive than he expected changed everything, leaving the woman he NEEDS on the verge of a breakdown.

He's done waiting and he'll do anything, even sacrifice everything he has to save her.

CHAPTER ONE

"I've got to go to work for a few hours and take care of a few things," Gabe spoke from the doorway, a frown marring his beautiful face.

Nina didn't respond. Instead, she continued to stare at the ceiling while lying in the bed. There was so much she could say, but none of it she knew how.

"Nina, did you hear me?"

Again, she said nothing. Gabe Michaels was the last person she wanted to talk to right now. She was broken, not stupid. The infuriating man had a thing for her. She got that now. But that didn't mean she'd let him into the pain trying to swallow her whole. At this point, she believed her whole life may be a joke.

Ever since Savannah Lewis had confessed to the murder of her husband, Nina's life had been in a tailspin.

"You're going to have to talk to me eventually. I've been patient and kind up to now, but that doesn't mean you get to act like a petulant child every day."

She slid her eyes toward the door where he currently stood filling it. Any time he walked into a room, he somehow dominated it. And it wasn't all about his huge six foot plus body that made women swoon to get his attention.

All the stuff she'd heard and occasionally seen at Purgatory Club explained some of what she sensed, but not all. Just because he liked to do kinky stuff in the bedroom, didn't explain why her insides quivered the moment she heard his voice.

For years they'd done a dance around their attraction with neither of them doing anything to take it very seriously. At least, that's what she'd thought. Apparently, Gabe did not agree.

He glanced at his watch. "I really do have to go now, but when I return the two of us are going to talk or else."

She almost broke her silence to demand what he meant by *or else*. When it came to Gabe, all bets were off. She'd heard the rumors for years. He liked women who obeyed and when they didn't, he enjoyed doling out punishment. And it appalled her that deep down she wanted to disobey him just to find out what he would do with her.

"Tori is on her way over so you might want to get up and get dressed. Maybe take a shower. I'm done letting you lay there feeling sorry for yourself." He took a step closer. "Get ready, Nina. I'm not kidding here."

She slid her gaze back to the ceiling trying to ignore the nervous butterflies in her stomach. There was something strangely appealing about bossy Gabe. Not that she'd ever tell him that. If he got a whiff that she might have submissive tendencies, he'd probably have her tied up across a spanking bench before she could get a word in edgewise.

When the front door closed behind Gabe and the house was once again engulfed in silence, Nina emerged from the oversized plush bed and padded into the bathroom.

He was right, of course. It was time for her to shake off this funk and get back to work. If Tori was coming here then she had no idea who was running the café.

She turned on the water in the shower the size of a carwash and waited for it to run hot. She stared into the mirror above the sink and cringed at the dark circles under her eyes. The results of not getting enough sleep these last couple of weeks were less than flattering and she wondered why Gabe continued to bother.

Unresolved attraction between them did not call for such devotion.

When the steam filled the room and fogged up the mirror, she stepped into the water and let the near scalding heat penetrate her skin. She hated this little girl lost feeling that had taken root inside her. In fact, she couldn't ever remember feeling quite this lost before.

Of course, that might have something to do with the fact that she couldn't remember certain times of her life. Particularly the months leading up to and directly after the death of Reverend Lewis. The man otherwise known as her bastard father.

She tried to push away those fruitless thoughts. No matter how hard she tried, she simply couldn't remember the night he died. Her brothers did though. They remembered the fire, the blood and even the knife supposedly buried in the good reverend's chest.

She dropped her forehead against the cool tile of the marble shower. Why the hell couldn't she stop thinking about it? If she couldn't remember, it was probably for good reason.

Tears burned at the back of her eyes. It wasn't that she missed her father or even that Savannah's confession really mattered to her.

What did matter were the looks of pity and suspicion she now saw across her brothers' faces.

They believed she was the killer, not Savannah.

The mere thought sickened her. First, the idea that she'd been the one to plunge a knife into her father's chest was ludicrous. What would have motivated her to do such a thing? The man had played little to no role in her life before his death. Even less since. The trust fund that her half-brother Mason had offered her had gone untouched.

Second, how could *they* think she'd done it? Her own brothers. The only men in her life besides Gabe she trusted.

Not that she could imagine Savannah doing

the deed either. The woman had spent the last decade in a psychiatric facility because she refused to speak. The more she thought about the situation, the more complicated it sounded. None of it made sense.

What could've prompted her stepmother to suddenly come forward after ten years of silence and claim responsibility for her husband's death?

Of course, if she had the answer to that she suspected everything would be clear. Except Mason had informed the family that Savannah refused to share any further details about that night.

Nina's head jerked up. Maybe the wrong person was asking. Just because she didn't want to open up to her lawyer or her son Tucker didn't mean...

Nina finished her shower and grabbed one of the plush bath sheets from the cabinet and wrapped her body in the soft cotton. If Savannah wouldn't talk to her son, maybe she would talk to her.

With an idea firmly planted in her mind, Nina hurriedly dressed in jeans and a sweater before shoving her feet into a pair of Converse. Despite the fancier clothes Gabe had offered her, she preferred her typical casual uniform. If it was good enough for the café, it could be good enough for a jail visit.

She grabbed a light jacket, a ponytail holder, sunglasses and the Carolina Panthers ball cap she'd found buried in the back of Gabe's closet. Not the best disguise in the world, but it would do in a pinch.

She had no idea if reporters still hovered around the courthouse that also happened to house the jail, but it was probably better to be safe than sorry.

For the first time in weeks she felt energized. The idea that Savannah could clear up her memory loss gave her a kernel of hope that she might come out okay on the other side of this nastiness after all. All she had to do was prove without a shadow of a doubt that she did not kill her father.

Before she could make it out the front door, the doorbell rang.

Shit.

She'd forgotten that Gabe told her Tori was on her way over. Now, she'd either have to try and get rid of her as quickly as possible or, she looked behind her at the back door that led to the garage, she could leave out the back way and call for an Uber once she got a couple of blocks away.

She nodded to herself. Yeah, that sounded like the better choice. Now that she had a plan, she wanted to go and visit Savannah before something else could get in her way.

Nina scooped up her cell phone and opened the back door while looking down at the screen. This caused her to miss the first step as she pitched forward only to crash into something that blocked her way. That something she recognized instantly by the scent of the cologne he wore. She swore softly and looked up, only to come face-to-face with Gabe.

"Going somewhere?" he asked.

She hesitated a fraction too long and his eyes narrowed down at her.

"Fresh air," she said, without elaborating any further. First rule of lying was to give them as little detail as possible. "I thought you were going to work." Second rule of lying was to deflect by changing the subject.

"I was. But something told me I was needed here more. That and the fact Tori messaged me to let me know you are not answering the door."

Nina sighed. "Oh for Christ's sake. It's been like two minutes."

He frowned down at her. "Actually, it's been more like twenty-five. She was starting to get worried."

"I was in the shower. Is that somehow against the Gabe rules?"

His right eyebrow arched. "The Gabe rules?"

"That's what it feels like. You appear to have a whole set of rules you expect everyone to follow and especially me. And from my experience if it looks like a duck, acts like a duck and feels like a duck, well then, I guess it's a duck."

He pushed into the house forcing her to take a step back. "I'm some sort of a duck now?"

"It's a metaphor, genius."

He took another step closer and removed her sunglasses. "And what is it a metaphor for? Friend? Caregiver? Babysitter? Or maybe lover?"

His use of the word lover came out on the sexy low rumble that never failed to send a shiver down her spine. But it was his fingers pulling at the holder wrapped around her hair that really caught her attention.

Any time he touched her, it managed to

scramble her brains until she couldn't think straight.

"More like tyrant," she said on a breathless gasp. This was exactly why she needed to get away from him. The more time she spent with him, the more her resolve weakened. "What are you doing?"

"Removing this silly disguise. If you want to go out, you don't need it."

There were a lot of things she wanted whenever she was around him. That was part of the problem. The longer she stayed the more she wanted to give him and she feared that more than anything. Hence the silence.

As long as she stayed withdrawn, it kept him at bay.

"I'm going to work too," she finally said.

"I'm sure Tori will be happy to hear that. Maybe you should answer the door and talk to her. You can go together."

She cringed at his words. It had been wrong for her to rely on the other woman to run her cafe for this long. Now she was adding lies to the rest of her recent transgressions.

No! She didn't lie about wanting to go to the cafe. That was in the plan as her second stop. She just failed to mention her entire itinerary.

The pounding on the front door continued and she wondered whether that was Tori or her heartbeat frantically trying to get his attention.

"Why don't *we* answer the front door and you and Tori can discuss it?"

"Discussion is overrated. Why don't you let her know that I've gone to the cafe and I'll meet up with her there later?"

His eyes narrowed. "So where are you really going then?"

Nina sighed. Damned man was like a bloodhound. "I told you."

"Not everything you didn't. How about I rephrase my question. Where are you going first?"

She huffed out the air in her lungs and crossed her arms over her chest. "You are not the boss of me, nor are you my father. I do not need to report every move I make to you."

He laughed, a rich, deep sound that filled the room around them while also wrapping around her like a safe cocoon, making him a walking, talking distraction.

They hadn't had much occasion to laugh lately and she'd forgotten how much she liked the sound of his or how it so easily affected her by basically melting her insides.

"I promised your brothers that I would keep you out of trouble. And that's what I intend to do. If that means keeping tabs on you, so be it. Besides, haven't you learned by now that I like to get my way?"

"I'm not one of your many submissives, Gabe. I don't work like that and you know it. I swear. You and my brothers are power hungry and can't stand for a second to let someone else be in control, can you?" She didn't wait for a response. "That's your issue, by the way. Not mine." She took another deep breath before she continued. "I mean, don't get me wrong. I needed a place to hunker down and think for a while and I appreciate you helping me out with that. But I'm ready now to rejoin the world. I'm going home."

"Is that so?"

She nodded. "For sure."

"Okay, if everything is so great as you put it, let me ask you one question. If you can answer it, then I will let you go."

Her heartbeat sped up as she tried to imagine what one question he could possibly ask. What one thing could she tell him that would make him believe her?

"Did you kill Reverend Lewis?"

The shock of the question hit her across the face as violently as if he'd slapped her. She sucked in air and bent at the waist. *Please, this couldn't be happening.* Her chest suddenly ached with a pain so fierce she wanted to scream.

"That's what I thought."

His statement caught her off guard. Enough for her to raise up and stare daggers at him. Anger surged through her, pushing some of the hurt away. "That's what you thought? Are you freaking kidding me? What the hell, asshole? You took me in, you made me feel safe again and now this? I've had it. I'm not going to listen to any more conjecture or innuendo and I'm certainly not going to stand here and watch you doubt me. What kind of bullshit is that? I trusted you."

"No, you didn't," he replied as vehemently as she. "If you did, you wouldn't be sneaking out of my house right now. Or you wouldn't have stopped talking to me when you got scared. And you most certainly wouldn't be lying to me right now."

"I am not scared," she said. Although, if she was, she certainly wouldn't admit it. Deep down, in a place she refused to look, fear might be lurking. But at the moment, she was annoyed and that's where she'd live for now if that's what it took to get through the day. "And I wasn't sneaking. You left, I got up as *instructed* and now I'm leaving just as soon as you get out of my way."

"I didn't ask that question because I doubt you. I don't. In fact, I already know the answer."

She turned from looking over his shoulder and met his gaze. The clear blue ocean of his eyes gave her little clues to the man inside. For whatever reason, he learned long ago how to control his emotions. She guessed it was a Dom thing, but she also suspected there was more. That need to know him on some level she couldn't describe was what kept her coming back to him time and time again.

To a man she could never have.

"If you are so sure you know the answer, then why ask?"

"Because I wanted to see your reaction. You claim you're fine. You're not. I know the answer, but you do not. And that," he stroked his fingers down her cheek, "is why you are *not* fine. But if you'd let me, I can help. You just have to stop shutting me out. I am not them, Angel."

Nina shivered. So much of her wanted to give in. Especially when he called her 'Angel.' The husky tone it came out on melted her insides. Oh, how she wanted to keep leaning on Gabe and allow him to take care of her. But she just couldn't. Her whole life had become about how well she stood on her own two feet. To backtrack now and rely on someone else any longer, it just didn't feel right. Not to mention unfair.

Gabe had his own life. As the manager of Purgatory Club and the Fire and Ice restaurant, he ran a tight, but busy ship.

He lived a life she couldn't be a part of.

She'd watched him too over the years. Yes, he played hard at the club and demanded more than most would give, but in the end, he always sacrificed what he needed for others.

She admired him for that, but it also broke her heart. He'd already given his fair share to this family. It wouldn't be right to ask him for more. It was time to end this cycle.

"Don't be so sure that you know who I am," she said. "If I can't remember, then you can't be sure. Whatever you're thinking, you're making assumptions and that's not fair. There's only one person who knows the truth and she's not talking."

His hand wrapped around the back of her neck and tugged her closer. So close she could feel his body heat along her front. She closed her eyes and allowed that warmth to comfort her one last time. She couldn't help herself.

"You're wrong, Angel. There is one other person and she is standing right here."

His insistence that she could remember scraped against her pride. "You think I haven't tried? No matter how many times I go back over that time in my life, it's blank. No, we have to get the truth from Tucker's mother. There's just no other way."

"It's all about trust, Nina. If you can let go of your stubborn pride and allow someone else to take control, your memories could come back. If you want them to, that is."

She bristled against his suggestion. "What's that supposed to mean? You think I'm doing this on purpose?" She'd about had it with this conversation. She needed to escape.

He sighed. "That's not what I'm saying at all. What I am saying is that I believe you're at an impasse. You can't do this on your own. Now, you could go the therapist route or maybe hypnosis."

She wrinkled her nose at his suggestions. "I can't do that. Are you crazy?"

He nodded. "Agreed. We both know the situation is far too tenuous and explosive to be discussed with strangers. That's why I have another proposal."

Nina bit her lip. She had an idea where this was going and it was making her nervous.

"Maybe we should talk about this later," she said, looking wistfully at the door over his shoulder.

"Look at me, Nina. This is serious and it's effecting your life. This big plan of yours to bury your head in the sand isn't working. Tucker, Mason, and Levi aren't going away. They are concerned about you. They are going to keep pushing."

"They think I killed our father. How do you think that makes me feel? What is it about me that makes everyone think I'm capable of such a thing? I'm not *that* aggressive."

Gabe chuckled, the soft sound sliding against her skin. "Babe, you can be. But you're right, that doesn't make you a killer. But bad things happen to good people and it makes them do things they normally wouldn't do."

The way he said that and the look in his eyes as he did made her think he spoke from experience. What did that mean? Did he have secrets, too? Her big idea to get out of the house and try to talk to Savannah was beginning to deflate. The more he pushed at her, the more she wanted to avoid the truth.

"Okay, I'll bite. What exactly is it that you want me to do? How do you propose I get my memories back without Savannah's help?"

He drew his lips into a thin, serious line. He also took another step closer, putting him well into her personal space.

"Submit to me. And by submit, I am not talking about sex. Although that could happen, too."

She started to protest and he held up his hand to stop her.

"No, let me finish. What I'm asking for is not simple and it is most definitely not easy. You've blocked old memories that are obviously traumatic. If you truly submit to me and learn to trust me, I believe we can unlock them."

"If you aren't talking about sex, then what are you talking about? I thought that's what the whole thing meant to you. I assumed taking control gave you pleasure." Her last sentence came out a little too breathless, but it was impossible to stay neutral with this man anytime the topic of sex hit the table.

Sex with Gabe... While out of the question, the idea fueled her fantasies and had for years.

A small smile curved his lips. "I do enjoy being

in control, but the real pleasure comes from the submissive and her desire to give me that control. For you, Nina, it can still be about pleasure, because that's normal when someone gets so deep inside your head that you temporarily let go. But make no mistake, the goal will be to help you break down the walls that are holding you back. Which leads us back to the only question left. Are you willing and ready to do whatever it takes to get to the truth?"

CHAPTER TWO

*G*abe studied her reactions looking for the little signs that would give him the answers he sought. To his surprise, she stayed calm, giving away no subtle signs of emotional turmoil hiding just below the surface.

With her body elegantly held straight, but her arms loose at her side and her lips closed, but not firmly pressed together she'd made it impossible for him to read her.

"Can I go now?" she asked.

He narrowed his eyes. Her constant need to avoid conflict concerned him. Every time someone asked her a hard question or one she didn't know the answer to, she deflected. Or worse, ran.

"Will you at least think about my proposal?"

"With baited breath," she said, sarcasm dripping from every syllable.

He shook his head. Her insolent attitude didn't help matters and he was beginning to lose patience, something he normally never did. It didn't help that his hand itched to spank her until he got his point across. A little time in subspace might finally allow her to see the truth.

He sighed. Those thoughts weren't going to get him anywhere. Which left him with only one course of action for now.

Facing the fact he wasn't going to make any headway with her at the moment, he stepped aside and motioned for her to go. Maybe some fresh air would do her good.

Except when she walked past him, he caught her looking at the screen of her cell phone at a familiar car service, which made a sudden surge of anger rise inside him.

"Don't even go there, Nina. You do not *need* a stranger to take you wherever it is you want to go. Your Cherokee is still parked outside and the keys are in the key case next to the garage door. Or I can drive you."

"How did you—? Never mind. I don't want to know. I'll drive myself." She turned and practically skipped down the stairs without another word, stopping only long enough to grab the keys and disappear through the door.

"Say hello to Savannah for me," he said to the empty room.

It wasn't easy watching her go. Not when part of him wanted nothing more than to continue hiding her from the world. He had a feeling it wouldn't take much for the situation with her family to spiral out of control.

She also wasn't the only one still in the dark. Mason had told him very little, keeping everything close to the vest as usual. And the details from Nina had come soaked in tequila, so it was hard to tell fact from fiction at this point.

He crossed the foyer and opened the front door to an irritated Tori standing on the other side.

"Was that Nina? I just saw her Jeep go down the driveway."

He nodded. "Might as well come in. I caught her trying to sneak out the back door."

"You just let her go? Is that a good idea right now? Is she going to the café? What about the—? Maybe I should just meet her there."

"I doubt you'll find her there, at least not right away. She claimed that's where she was headed, but little Miss Secretive wasn't telling the truth. I've known her long enough to know when she's hiding something."

"I don't understand. I thought she wasn't communicating? Do we need to go after her?"

Gabe narrowed his eyes and pursed his lips. "What do you think? She's not one to be managed."

Tori laughed and shook her head. "No, she's not. But I'm going to guess that if you've let her go out on her own like this, then you or Mason are having her followed and that wherever she is going the two of you will probably know before she does."

He pinched his lips and said nothing. He felt no need to confirm or deny that accusation. Yes, they might be called controlling, but more importantly, they were being cautious. The situation at the moment felt a little like sitting on a keg of dynamite that hadn't decided whether it was going to blow or not.

Gabe led Tori into the kitchen without bothering to answer. Her relationship with Levi meant that she had a pretty good idea what it was like to be part of this family and the women seemed to know their men well.

"Breakfast?" he waved his hand over the buffet

that had been laid out while he was gone to the office. He was surprised Nina had not noticed.

Before she could answer him, the doorbell sounded again.

"Let me guess," she said. "I was lured over here this morning as cover." She glanced around at the place settings at the breakfast table, counting each one. "One, two, three, four, five, six, seven and eight. Jesus, that's the whole family. Were you planning some sort of an intervention? Except now the interventionee has left the building?"

Gabe shrugged. "Don't look at me. This was definitely not my idea."

Before Tori could ask any more questions, they were interrupted by the arrival of the rest of the family.

Levi walked up to his woman with a wide grin across his face. "Hey babe," he said, kissing her on the cheek.

"You could have told me about this, you know," she said.

"Nah, what fun would that be? I thought you like surprises."

Tori whispered something to Levi that Gabe couldn't make out as they crossed the room, but he guessed when they got home alone the fireworks would go off. Those two had a hard time keeping their hands off of each other on a good day. Add in a little conflict and they combusted.

Gabe shook Mason's hand and then shook his head. "I think your sister must have radar when it comes to your interference."

Tucker joined them next. "Why's that?"

"Because for the first time in days, your sister left the house."

"What?" Mason exploded. "And you just let her leave? Where did she go? Why didn't you call me?"

Rebecca, Mason's lovely submissive, laid her hand gently on his arm. "I'm sure she's fine. She probably saw this coming a mile away. She's no slouch, you know."

"Maybe she's tired of your suspicions." Tucker's directed comment toward Mason fell like a bomb in a deathly quiet room.

"Oh no. No fucking way. You all are not blaming this all on me." Mason turned to Gabe. "I'm not the only one who agreed this was a good idea."

Levi stepped between all of them. "No one's blaming anyone. Push come to shove, we all agreed to this."

"I didn't agree," Tori said. "And I'm not so sure I would have. Nina is her own woman. If there is anything I know about her, it's the fact that she can stand on her own two feet. Last week you all agreed that she needed some time to think. Now all of a sudden, you want to gang up on her?" She shook her head. "This family is in turmoil and some shit is still going to hit the fan, but arguing with each other is going to get you exactly nowhere."

Gabe hid the smile that wanted to come out. He'd always liked Tori, but especially now more than ever. He missed her working in the club, as did the customers. She may not have been a true Domme at heart, but she had a gift with people nonetheless.

Gabe cleared his throat. "Why don't we get something to eat, sit down and put our heads together? This isn't just about Nina, is it? What's really at stake?"

All three brothers glanced at each other at his question, an easy tell that there was a lot more to the story to still come out.

"I'm worried about Nina. Do you know where she's going?" The frown across Mason's face made Gabe remember how much worry and stress he carried for his family. Sometimes he wondered if they even realized how much he did for them. Most only saw the hard exterior, but Gabe had spent a lot of time with the man and he knew just how deep his loyalty to family went.

"We should know soon where she's headed," Gabe informed them. Not that he needed confirmation.

"So you *are* having her followed?" Tori asked.

"I'm taking precautions." He didn't feel the need to elaborate beyond that. Yes, they were her family and had a right to be concerned about her, but this was his job now, whether they liked it or not.

She needed someone other than a blood relation to look out for her. Someone who cared about her in different ways.

Fuck that. Not someone. Him.

He'd bided his time for a long fucking time and he was tired of waiting. The call from Tori a few weeks ago about Nina being sloppy drunk and sobbing in her storeroom office had not only been a wakeup call, but a final straw.

He'd taken control. Something he wasn't about to give up now that he had it.

Everyone gathered around the table and picked out seats. Tucker and Maggie at the far end with

Levi and Tori down one side and Mason and Rebecca the other. That left the end of the table for him and one other seat to his right for Nina.

He stood back and watched. Did they even realize they were his family, too? Tucker leaned into his wife and whispered something in her ear while his hand protectively cradled her baby bump. Their family would soon grow.

He felt the corners of her lips turn up in a subtle smile. These assholes had somehow managed to turn the most tragic day in his life into the beginning of something new.

His parents had been killed in a car accident back when he was in college on their way to his first football game. A truck driver had fallen asleep at the wheel and crossed over the center line at the precise moment they were about to pass the truck.

All parties involved were killed instantly.

As the only child of two only children who'd waited to start a family until almost middle age, he'd been left with no one.

Except the three men sitting at his table right now.

For some unknown reason, young men he barely knew other than as fellow players on their college football team where he was the low ranking freshman who spent most of his time riding a bench, scooped him up at the morgue that night after he'd been pulled from the game by state highway patrol to identify dead bodies. They never left him alone again.

He'd become a part of their unusual friendship. He'd never quite understood how the three of them had been so close until years later when Mason had revealed to him that the three of them were half-brothers.

At the time, he hadn't elaborated and it had been quite a few more years before he'd discovered their connection was none other than the deceased, but still infamous preacher, Reverend Lewis.

Now, that had made a lot of sense.

It at least explained why they kept their lives so secret.

By then they were all long-time business partners in the Purgatory Club, a goth and fetish night club, with a private membership component that took up the third floor of the building. There, many of the city's elite and often wealthy clientele could indulge in what many would consider sexual deviance.

The brothers had introduced him to kink by including him on some of their weekend excursions into the city, one thing had led to another and now he ran the club for them. Unlike them, he did not need to keep his sexual proclivities quiet. Instead, he'd indulged quite publicly for many years.

And it was precisely those activities that had kept him eternally single.

"Gabe, you going to just stand there and watch us or are you going to join us?" Levi asked.

"Yeah, Gabe," an all too familiar female voice from behind him said. "Are you going to join them?"

CHAPTER THREE

Nina had stood just inside the front door while she listened to her family discuss her. She hadn't gotten far when the realization of just what these idiots were up to had soaked into her desperate mind.

That information alone had forced her to high-tail it back here as quickly as possible.

Admittedly, she'd rushed through the house this morning with a single-minded focus—getting out before Gabe returned.

But somewhere along the way as she sped through the kitchen and out the garage door, her mind had registered a full buffet table covered with food. It had just taken more time than usual for her brain to process it.

There had been enough to feed a small army, or her family.

With her memory of Tori pounding on the front door and Gabe mysteriously returning after having just left for what should have been hours had all percolated in her mind until she was ready to see it.

Gabe turned and looked at her, surprise crossing his features.

"I'm surprised you came back."

She shrugged her shoulders. "I'm pretty surprised myself. More like shocked actually that you'd do this to me. An intervention, really?" She turned to the rest of the group. "That's what this is, right?"

"Why don't you join us and we can discuss it?" Mason leveled his 'I'm a big bad Dom' gaze on her and even lowered his voice like she'd heard him do with Rebecca.

That only served to make her angrier. "There's nothing to discuss," she said through gritted teeth.

"Nina," Gabe started.

She whirled back to him. "Please don't Nina me right now. This whole situation is such a betrayal of trust, I don't even know where to get started. So unless you want to push me into saying something we'll both regret, I suggest you stop now."

His eyebrows climbed his forehead and she could imagine how shocked he was to be talked to like that. Especially given how obedient she'd been these last few weeks.

That went for all of them. The men in this room were so overdone on testosterone, they couldn't stand not being in charge at all times.

Well, they were just going to have to suck it up for once. When it came to her life, she was in charge, not them.

"She's right," Tori spoke up from her seat and all eyes turned to her. "Now hold on before you all go off on me, too. Hear me out. This whole family has been under a lot of stress lately. Lots of changes have happened both good and bad and it seems we're putting too much pressure on Nina to be the one to take responsibility."

"Tori," Levi warned.

"What? I'm not wrong. We're all being convinced to believe that if Nina faces up to whatever is stressing her out that somehow everything will be magically better. But maybe it's not that simple. She's not the only one with answers, you know."

"I agree." For the first time since she'd entered the room, Tucker spoke up.

Nina turned her gaze to him, the face she'd been avoiding the most. He'd been the closest thing she'd had to a real brother growing up. All those years of his father coming to her house, all but ignoring her and it had been Tucker's shoulder she cried on when he left.

In fact, her sneaking into his big house on the lake had become such a regular thing, he kept his window unlocked all the time just in case.

He knew more than any of them how frustrating and painful her non-relationship with their father had been. Now, he too thought she'd killed him. That killed *her*.

The fact she couldn't remember the details of that night made her want to pull her hair and scream. Why couldn't her brain cooperate and just let her remember? Then she could shut them all up once and for all.

"Do you think I did it, too?" She interrupted whatever he'd planned to say.

He stared back at her. His mouth now set in a grim line, his nostrils flared as he took a deep breath. Next to him, Maggie had a death grip on his arm as if trying to stop him or hold him back or something.

Nina closed her eyes against the wave of emotion slamming into her. He didn't need to answer the question. It was written all over his face. Why she'd forced him to affirm what she suspected had been stupid on her part.

She opened her eyes and once again surveyed the entire group around the table. Her brothers, their wives and/or girlfriends, although they preferred to call them submissives. Maggie and Tucker had run off to Vegas and gotten married. Now they were expecting their first child.

Maggie had been a professor until a big scandal had gotten in her way and drove her back home and into the arms of her first love. However, her research into the BDSM lifestyle had eventually proven useful when she'd begun receiving invitations to teach seminars here and there at some of the big colleges across the country.

Levi had returned after more than ten years away and hooked up with Tori. Although they hadn't set a wedding date yet, she expected something soon. Tori's daughter Hannah wouldn't stop questioning them about it and Levi had fallen so head over heels for both of them he wasn't about to make either of them wait long.

Mason on the other hand, what a mess. He'd somehow gotten mixed up with a reporter named Rebecca, who despite her poor choice of profession was far sweeter than a grump like him deserved. He'd recently rescued her from living in her car and if not for the current drama surrounding their family, he'd have probably disappeared with her by now.

Despite being the CEO of their father's conglomerate, he hated public attention and guarded their secrets like a crazed mad dog.

Her family.

What a joke.

"You all still believe I'm guilty, don't you?" Her shoulders sagged under the weight of it all. The idea that every one of them assumed her guilt had taken root inside her and she'd allowed it to fester for weeks by not talking to them.

"It's not that simple, Nina. The circumstances that night..."

"How can you say that when none of you know the circumstances? You got there too late, remember?"

Tucker visibly winced at her words.

With tears threatening to spill, Nina regretted returning to this house. She'd made her escape. She should have kept going.

As if reading her distress, a familiar warm hand touched the small of her back and without thought she automatically leaned into it, once again closing her eyes.

Gabe. Always her rock.

A man who didn't take no for an answer, but didn't push her for something she couldn't give either.

A different kind of guilt and regret rose up, threatening to consume her. She could hardly remember a time when he wasn't in her life. So much so that she couldn't even pinpoint the moment she'd fallen in love with him.

Just that she had.

Not that it mattered. If there was one lesson she'd managed to learn over and over in her life, it was that love definitely wasn't enough to conquer all. Not family, not childhood, and certainly not death.

"Nina, we have to know what happened. Surely, you understand that. My mother is sitting in jail. She refuses to tell us anything. You are our

only hope to save her. Victor needs something—
anything—that might help."

"You think I don't know that?" she choked on a
sob, barely able to look at Tucker. "If I could
remember I would tell you!"

"Shhh, Nina. It's okay." Gabe hooked her waist
with his free arm and turned her toward him,
tucking her into his side.

"No. it's not," she mumbled into his shoulder.

"Nina—"

"Shut up, Mason," Gabe said.

"Excuse—"

"No, seriously," Gabe's tone hardened. "I let
you talk me into this against my better judgment
and all it's done is hurt her. This isn't the way."

Nina pushed at his side, forcing herself to let
go of her usual Gabe safety net. "You don't have to
talk for me. I'm not a child anymore."

Gabe's eyes narrowed on her and a chill
swept across her skin. "I definitely know you're
not a child." He scrubbed his hands across his
face. "Believe me, I *know*. But you do *need* protection. Wait—" He held up his hand. "I know you
want to argue with me, you always do, but for
once just listen." He turned to the rest of her
family. "All of you need to listen. This is a serious

situation and trying to force it isn't going to work. It takes time."

"We don't have—"

"Too fucking bad. Look, I get how you feel. You all love your family. No matter how strange it is. But in this, I am *her* advocate and only hers."

"I think you're overstepping your bounds. This is a family situation."

Nina winced on behalf of Gabe at Mason's words. His need to bully his way through a negotiation was going to be the death of him one of these days. Either someone would get fed up and do something drastic or all that anger would make him drop dead of a heart attack.

"This is my house," Gabe said. "If you don't want me to be a part of your family, you're always welcome to leave."

Levi stood. "Okay, we all need to take a breath here. This is getting out of hand. Gabe, of course you're part of our family. That's not what Mason meant." He ran his hand over his face before he continued. "Tensions are high. No one's getting enough sleep. The situation sucks. That makes people say things they don't really mean." He turned and faced her. "Nina, no one is accusing you of anything. That bastard got what he deserved and then some. In fact, I wish it could have been me. He cost me my mother. Hell, he cost us all so much. In that respect, death might have been too easy for him."

Nina wanted to cry for Levi and his mother. Her suicide had driven him over the edge and as far away from North Carolina as he could get. They were lucky he'd bothered to return at all.

"I know," she whispered. "That's why this is so hard. If I could remember, I swear I'd tell you. I've tried everything these last few weeks. Meditation, breathing and memory exercises. I've even thought about hypnosis."

"What?" Gabe twisted her so she faced him. "Why the hell would you do that? And with who? I thought we talked about this? Are you crazy?"

She sighed. "Apparently so."

He shook his head. "Sorry. Poor choice of words. But what the hell, woman?" He reached up and cupped her cheek. "You have to be careful. You can't just let your guard down with anyone. There could be repercussions."

Nina gritted her teeth until the urge to sob all over him receded. "That's the problem. I *can't* let my guard down with anyone." She lowered her voice. "Not even my family."

CHAPTER FOUR

*G*abe had to clench his jaw to keep control of his temper. He'd have to have a serious talk with his security team about watching her closer. He'd not heard a word about anyone he didn't know visiting with Nina since he'd brought her home.

"Who were you planning to talk to, Nina?" While Gabe asked the question, he could practically hear the tension vibrating off of Mason. It was a minor miracle he'd not lost it over this little revelation.

Between Nina's incessant need to run and hide from her problems, and Mason's drive to railroad everyone into his way of thinking, they were all walking on a bit of a tightrope at the moment.

"One of my customers at the cafe is a psychotherapist. I've known her for years and I trust her. Plus she's bound by her professional oath to keep everything she learns about her clients private. Maybe she could help."

Mason snorted. "You are way too naive for your own good. And clearly, you need a better keeper. What the hell, Gabe? I thought you had this?"

Gabe was getting close to choking the life out of Mason if he didn't shut the hell up. Boss or no didn't matter when it came to the woman in his arms.

"That's nasty even for you, Mason," Rebecca said.

Gabe smiled at the woman. He didn't know Mason's submissive very well, but at the moment he was damned happy with her. If Mason didn't have someone in his life who would stand up to him when he really needed it, they were all screwed. While his intentions were solid, he'd still try to run roughshod over them all.

Someone had to keep his ass in line. And he was getting tired of that particular game.

"Yes, Mason. That was nasty," Nina choked. "And uncalled for. Where's all the love and support you've promised me all these years? Or does that come only when it's convenient for you?"

"Jesus, Nina." Mason sucked in a breath, a brief flash of pain covering his face. "You make me out like a monster when all I've done is try to help. I don't want to see you punished any more than Savannah. Neither one of you deserve this shit."

"Then don't blame any of this on Gabe. He's done nothing but try to help."

Despite his best effort to school his emotions, Gabe's chest puffed up and a slight smile pulled at the corners of his mouth. He rather enjoyed watching Nina defend him even though he didn't need it. Maybe the new plan of getting her to submit to him that had been forming in his mind over the last couple of days had a chance after all. If she had feelings for him, then maybe he could help her.

Over the years, there had been more than one look across a room or a violently shared kiss in a weak moment that gave him hope. But he'd never gotten past the major roadblock she continued to keep between them.

His sexual preferences.

Hell, who was he kidding? His preference to be in control, or rather to be given control by the woman under his care extended well beyond the bedroom.

These last few weeks of them living together proved that. He'd allowed her a lot of leeway in her grief, but when push came to shove and her health was at risk, he maintained total control.

And she'd responded to it every damn time. In fact, he hadn't thought of it like that until now. But his feisty little house guest might have more submissive tendencies than she realized.

"It's okay, Angel. He can say whatever he needs to. If he crosses a line I don't like, I'll just kick him out of my house."

"You're not supposed to call me that, remember?" she whispered, probably hoping no one heard her. But by the look on all their faces, it was clear they did. And now they were all more curious than ever.

Mason shook his head. "This is definitely getting out of hand."

Gabe didn't disagree. There were so many players involved in this little drama that he couldn't keep their stories straight. He'd known all along that they hadn't told him everything. A fact he hadn't fought because he wanted to learn the truth with Nina.

She deserved someone on her side not completely colored by her brother's opinions.

He lowered his lips to her ear and whispered back. "I couldn't help it. You were being so sweet. Maybe I should start calling you 'Tiger' instead."

A half snort/half laugh bubbled out of her so unexpectedly she slapped her hand across her mouth to stop it. Goddamn, her reactions to him were often priceless. How she couldn't see how good they'd be together made no sense to him. This arm's length thing was getting old.

He meant that metaphorically of course, because she'd been in his arms almost day and night since he'd found her drunk on nearly an entire bottle of tequila in her cafe storeroom. After babbling something about murder and blood and betrayal, she'd clung to him like a lifeline, barely letting go until this morning.

That realization jerked his thoughts. What had happened this morning to change things? God, why did he agree to this stupid breakfast intervention? He needed to get these people out of his house so he could have a serious talk with Nina.

"Call me 'Tiger' and I'll show you a wild cat by clawing your eyes out first."

His hands tightened on her waist. The fire in

her words made his body stand up and sing. Especially his cock. He'd become almost monk-like these last few weeks and right then, in the most inappropriate moment, his body told him that shit had to end.

"Is that a threat or a promise?" he asked. "Because I'm about to take you up on that offer."

"Why are you two not taking this seriously?" Tucker asked, pulling him back into the fact her entire family sat around a table not two feet away from him. And he didn't have to turn and look to know Mason glared at him. He could easily imagine his face turning red with anger over the blatant flirting going on between him and Nina.

"Trust me, I am very serious. But this was a mistake." Whatever had woken her this morning had clicked something inside her. He had a hunch she was finally ready to move on to something more productive. "Yep," he nodded. "A mistake, but a worthy one since we've learned it wasn't necessary. We can all move on."

"Move on to what?" Levi asked, clear skepticism evident in his voice. "We don't have a lot of time. The grand jury is set to convene soon to determine whether or not Savannah should stand trial for murder."

He couldn't think about that. While he wasn't going to admit it out loud, his priorities had nothing to do with whether Mrs. Lewis was guilty or not.

He squeezed Nina's waist in a show of reassurance. He didn't want her to falter now.

"Then I suggest you work on getting your mother to open up. Her memory appears to be intact and she's simply refusing to cooperate. Someone needs to find out why. In the meantime, Nina and I will start working together to see what we can uncover."

"We will?" Nina looked up at him with a mix of fear and defiance. God, it was good to see this side of her again. He'd harbored real concerns that she'd been broken one too many times.

Tori snorted before she stood with her plate and walked in the direction of the buffet. "I can't take this anymore. This is like a tragic game of 'who's on first' that is getting painful to watch. I'm hungry and need food to keep up."

"Oh, hell yes. I second that." Maggie jumped to her feet, rubbing her little belly. "This baby needs sustenance."

After that, the room exploded as everyone moved and talked at once. With Nina watching him closely, everyone else around them faded to a dull roar. He absently heard the dishes clang as well as movement all around him, but none of it held his focus.

That honor remained with her.

"Do you trust me?" he asked.

"I thought I did, until this." Her eyelids lowered and her mouth turned down in a slight frown.

"I didn't betray you. I knew this little stunt would have little effect on your memory."

"Then why do it? I feel sick standing here trying not to think about what each of them thinks when they look at me."

"Oh, Angel." He pulled her closer and wrapped his hand around the back of her head. "Don't do that. They love you. I mean, we all know this family is as unconventional as it gets, but that doesn't seem to have any effect on the bond you all share. Even Mason means well."

She started to protest and he placed a finger at her lips. "Trust me. They would not go to this much trouble if they didn't care. Trust me and trust them. Ultimately, we all just want to protect you."

"They go too far." She frowned.

He smiled and pressed his finger against the downturn of her mouth. "Of course they do. That's what family does. There's probably a law written somewhere that requires families to be giant pains in the asses."

This time she laughed and he soaked the delicate sound in. He'd missed that from her more than he'd realized. That thought made him want to kiss her. That and the fact she was practically pressed against his body with her lips only inches away from his.

"You can let her go now," Tucker said, coming up behind him.

He ignored his friend, giving Nina one last squeeze before releasing her. He'd chosen to keep his back to Tucker for the moment due to his current raging desire to punch him for interrupting. They'd been having a moment and those were precious and far between these days.

"Go eat, Angel. We'll talk later."

To his surprise, she didn't argue or complain about him calling her 'Angel' again in front of her brother.

"Are you really okay?" he overheard Tucker ask her as he backed away. He turned away from them before she could answer, preferring to give them some privacy. He sensed something between them that needed to be resolved.

Over the years, he'd believed that Mason was

the one who had the power to cut her the deepest. They'd certainly bickered often enough. But her direct questioning of Tucker at the table when she'd arrived hinted at a different story.

His angel had so many layers and he couldn't wait to start working his way through them.

"Here."

Gabe looked up to find Tori holding out a plate of food to him.

"You need to eat too, you know. You've been working yourself to the bone trying to take care of everyone else. Who's taking care of you?" she asked.

"You're worried about me? I'm touched."

She shrugged. "I notice these things. Nina is hurting something fierce, but so are you. I thought she would have come around to you already."

He followed Tori's gaze to find Nina and Tucker still engaged in a quiet, but uncomfortable looking conversation. "She's stubborn. Doesn't open up much either. It's not going to be easy."

Tori laughed. "Sounds like someone else I know."

"Why don't you tell me how you really feel?"

She laughed harder. "You know I call 'em like I

see 'em. You two seem to belong together. Even if she'll never admit it."

"Hmm. Maybe. There is also such a thing as beating a dead horse."

She guffawed. "Oh please, don't even pretend you're thinking about giving up. I'd bet my last dollar you'd die trying. Giving up is not in your nature."

Tori definitely had a point. He'd waited this long and he could almost taste the essence of Nina on his tongue. They certainly had no shortage of chemistry. But until she got her past where it belonged—in the past—they'd remain in limbo.

He surveyed the room. First, he had some guests to get out of his house. As everyone gathered at the table and ate their food, the conversation remained lively. Some mundane topics were bandied about and then punctuated with more serious side notes about the future.

For Gabe, he couldn't focus on anything other than the next step with Nina. How many years had she denied interest in him or his proclivities? Yet, how many nights had she come to Purgatory with her girlfriends dressed to the nines and tempting his guests with her lovely body and sharp, intelligent eyes?

Why? He had so many questions without answers and he was well past ready to get them.

"Get out," he said.

Everyone gathered ceased their discussions and turned their gazes toward him.

"Excuse me?" Mason said. "I think you and I need to have a—"

"I said get out," he repeated, uncaring about protocol or niceties at the moment. He turned to Nina. "It's time for everyone to go. You and I have work to do." He left the room without saying another word.

CHAPTER FIVE

*A*n hour later Nina stood on the threshold of Gabe's office, not sure she wanted to go any farther. The dark, wood door stood slightly ajar, as if he'd left it that way just for her. It shouldn't surprise her that he'd wait for her to come to him. He had that way about him that managed to get him what he usually wanted without saying a word.

His oddball demand that forced everyone to leave abruptly had come out of left field and thrown her for a loop. And yet, something about the way he'd looked at her on his way out of the room had her going along with it.

Only once everyone left, she'd spent her time cleaning up the dining room and kitchen instead of confronting Gabe. Her thoughts and emotions were still all over the map and she'd been unable to get his suggestion that she submit to him out of her mind.

She thought she was ready to try anything that could help her get past the missing memories, but what he was asking...

She had a lot more at stake than simply memories of the past. She had her heart to consider. And the idea of being that vulnerable to him scared the holy hell out of her.

She turned away from the doorway and started back up the hallway to the kitchen and stopped halfway to her destination. Hiding away wasn't the answer either. That had gotten old. But what could she do? Was there some sort of compromise that would give them both what they needed while protecting her heart?

Not likely.

"What's wrong?" Gabe's strong voice filled the hallway from behind her.

Crap. Her stomach tightened.

"Nothing," she said, without turning around.

"Then why are you pacing up and down the hallway?"

"How did you—?"

"This is my house. I know its creaks and moans by heart. I can hear your footfalls every time you approach my office."

Nina rolled her eyes, grateful he could see her face. "I didn't mean to disturb you," she mumbled under her breath.

Gabe sighed long and loud. "You never disturb me. In fact, I've been waiting for you. The point of kicking everyone else out was so we could spend some time alone talking, not for you to play house-keeper. But we both know you already knew that."

"You were rude," she said as she gripped her fingers hard in an attempt to control her need to fidget.

"I'm willing to bet they were all over it by the time they got home. Well, maybe Mason will stew over it a little longer and then try to kick my ass, but he worries too much about everything."

"Maybe they are over it, but still. Talk about awkward."

He took several steps closer until she could feel his heat radiating against her back. "I needed to be alone with you."

"Why?" she asked, although she immediately regretted it. If he was planning to pull her closer, she wasn't sure she could say no. Staying with him, in his house, might have been a fatal mistake after all. Keeping herself closed off from him all this time had not been easy.

Sadness suddenly clouded her thoughts. Falling for Gabe now would not end well for her. Didn't matter if she was already there. Taking the next step with him, even for all the right reasons, would forever alter their chance at just a friendship.

Her belly fluttered as she imagined living here permanently and all that would entail.

"I wanted to be alone because I got the sense that something changed for you this morning. When I left you seemed the same as always, but then something happened. You woke up. What happened?"

She wrinkled her forehead. "What? I mean, nothing happened this morning. I just got tired of feeling sorry for myself and doing nothing."

"Look at me."

She froze, her muscles locking into place. Why did she suddenly think that was a really bad idea?

Despite that, she began to slowly turn. She jumped, taken aback, when she realized how close he actually was to her without her realizing. She breathed deep and closed her eyes momentarily to regain her equilibrium. Only, this close, all that accomplished was her getting a deep inhale of his scent. She sighed again.

He wore a subtle musky scented cologne that she really liked, but beyond that, he always smelled like Purgatory. Or maybe she just associated him with that. Either way, the deep, rich masculine scent of expensive leather mingled along her senses. She breathed deeper, taking more of it in. Leather, musk and something she could only describe as heat filled her lungs.

Gabe Michaels smelled like power. And to her shame, she liked it.

That instantaneous draw to someone else's power might as well be her kryptonite. That irresistible lure drew women like her in, robbing them of their ability to see or think straight. She only had to look at her mother to see its long-term effect. It had certainly been her downfall.

And yet, knowing all she knew about powerful men and their women, it still pulled at her.

"Tell me where you were going when you left and don't bother lying again. I can tolerate a lot of bullshit, but not lies. Especially from you."

His question jerked her from her thoughts and back to their conversation. "Why especially from me?" she asked, seemingly unable to stop asking the questions that were going to get her answers she couldn't handle.

"Because I care about you. And I need to trust in you as much as you need to trust in me. We can't have trust if you aren't willing to be honest with me."

She inwardly winced. "I didn't lie to be mean or evasive. I just wanted to do something on my own with the least amount of friction. I figured telling you that I wanted to talk to Savannah Lewis would end up in a big drama with you taking over and insisting I couldn't go alone."

His facial expression didn't change. Not a lick of surprise crossed his face. Nor did her sarcasm seem to surprise him.

"How'd you know anyway?" she asked.

He shrugged. "Call it a hunch. Or maybe just logic. Take your pick. I knew you weren't going to the cafe and it seemed the only other real option all things considered. If you were going to see someone else you would have said so."

She mulled over his thought process and conclusions. They made sense. For a minute she thought he'd had her followed or something.

Except she hadn't gotten far enough for anyone to know where she might be headed.

"I still want to talk to her."

"I'm sure you do. Although, it might not help. She seems to have answers she doesn't want to give."

"Why do you think that is? I mean why, after all this time, does she suddenly confess? It's weird, don't you think?"

He nodded. "It is. But you have to admit, this family is a bit on the weird side."

She almost smiled. "You're part of this family too, you know. That makes you just as weird as the rest of us."

He took another step closer and entered her personal space. "Maybe the weirdest of the bunch. Why else would I still be here?"

His voice lowered an octave on his last comment and she looked up at him through her lashes. Why did he have to be so beautiful? On top of that incredible voice and a tight body made for sin, which he kept covered by suits or leather almost all the time, he was also a dark-haired gorgeous devil.

Vibrant sapphire blue eyes stared down at her, making her squirm.

What else could explain such a perfect package but a pact with Satan? Her mind and gaze wandered to his thick, broad shoulders. He'd been a football player back in the day, just like her brothers and she could see why. With heavy muscles, an intelligent mind and determined attitude, he was nothing less than a walking, talking pitbull. She pitied anyone who came up against him for any reason.

They'd met not long after he graduated from college. Her brothers had talked about him nonstop and tried to introduce them sooner when he came around on the holidays and other school breaks. But she'd refused.

The early years after her father's death had not been easy. Just because she couldn't remember what happened that night didn't magically make the situation any easier for her. The man had been a hateful, negative influence on her life for so long.

"You have a lot going on in here." Gabe tapped the side of her head. "Care to share any of it?"

She tried to shake the encroaching melancholy that always came with remembering that time and failed. She considered his request and finally let out the breath she hadn't realized she'd been holding.

"Just thinking about when you became part of this family and how much of that I missed. Tucker and Mason talked about you all the time when you weren't around. Did you know that?"

He shook his head. "No. I was a little preoccupied trying to get through school. It wasn't the happiest time for me."

"Because of your parents," she whispered.

He nodded, reaching up to touch her cheek. Automatically she turned and pressed her lips to his hand. The need to comfort him overwhelmed her. How stupid of her to bring up that painful time.

"I'm sorry. I didn't mean to make you–"

"Don't be. Believe it or not, I do like remembering them. There were a lot of good memories."

She tentatively smiled. "I like that about you. You tend to go for the positives in life. You don't get mired down by the past."

He barked a rough laugh. "Don't put me up on a pedestal I can't live up to, Angel. Not everything about me is quite so easy going."

She knew that, too. Although she wasn't sure she understood it. A myriad of questions swirled in her mind because of it.

"Go ahead," he said.

"What?"

"I can tell you want to ask me something. So ask. If I have the answer, I will tell you. I keep talking about trust between us and that goes both ways. So ask the burning questions while you can. I may not always be this accommodating."

She hesitated, licking her lips. There were always questions, but that didn't means she wanted to hear the answers. Especially if she didn't like them.

"Scared?" he asked.

A little. But she wasn't about to admit that.

"I should ask you why you're so stubborn, but that would be a waste of a perfectly good question."

He laughed. "Probably for the same reasons you are."

She huffed out air, narrowing her eyes. Every time he called her stubborn her defenses automatically raised. That question definitely wouldn't get them anywhere.

"That's not what I wanted to know anyway."

He rubbed his thumb along her jawline, eliciting a tingle of excitement shuddering across her skin.

"I know it isn't, Angel. So ask the question you really want the answer to."

She started to argue and once again point out how infuriating he could be, but she stopped herself. They were going to get exactly nowhere if she couldn't be honest.

"Why BDSM? Why do you have to have that in your life? And why are you so sure it will help me?"

He didn't answer right away. Instead, he ran his finger along the seam of her lips until she parted them on a sigh.

"You ask that like you think there should be a simple cut and dry answer."

"It does seem straightforward. I mean a little kink here and there I get. It can be the spice of life or whatever. I've seen enough of it to at least get that part. But that's not what I've heard about you. Or Mason, or Tucker, or even Levi." She looked up at him. "But please don't elaborate on my brothers because I don't need any more pictures of them in my brain. I'd like to be able to maintain my friend-ships with Maggie, Tori and Rebecca without imagining them doing something weird for my brothers."

Gabe laughed, the rich deep sound filling the room. "Oh, Nina." He gently grasped her arms and pulled her against him. "You have so much to learn.

The fact you still think it's weird tells me so much more than words."

She resisted his hold because not doing so made her brains scramble. "No, that's not true. I've been to Purgatory. I've heard Maggie and Tori talk. Tori even told me about her former job as a pro Domme in your club. I think I've got a pretty good grasp on how kink works."

His smile faded away, making her sad to see it go. "Maybe you do understand the mechanics of kink, but you clearly don't understand the underlying emotional aspect of it. Otherwise, you wouldn't have asked me. Now hold on before you get all resistant again. Don't take that as a criticism because it's not how it was meant. You don't learn about what makes a man or a woman tick by osmosis or observation. It takes experience to truly understand. Until you've walked in the shoes, you can't know why even your best friend can't live without it from the Dom she loves. And even once you experience it and think you get it, that won't apply to everyone. We're all human. And we're complicated. What works for one person doesn't necessarily work for another."

She blinked when he finally took a breath, letting his words sink in. "Are you trying to tell me that I'm never going to understand why you need it in your life? That sounds like a convenient way to not answer the question."

He shook his head, his lips compressing in a thin line. "I didn't say that at all. My only point is that we'd be better served if I showed you."

Nina tried to take a step back, but Gabe held her still. "No, Angel. You asked the question. You opened the door. Let me show you."

She shook her head. "You're right. I am afraid."

"Tell me exactly what you are afraid of. Is it that you think I will hurt you or that I want to?"

She shrugged.

"I think you know better than that. While there can be pain involved most of the time, it is either for your own good or for pleasure. A lot of pleasure, I might add."

She could feel her heartbeat growing frantic as panic welled inside her at the thought of what kind of pleasure Gabe wanted to give. "What do you mean for my own good?" She gasped, unable to hide the anxiety filling her.

Gabe shook his head at the same time he lifted his hand to stroke her cheek. "Easy. We're just talk-ing. I am not going to force you to do anything you don't want. But I wasn't kidding when I told you that I think it could help. For one, you're wound too tight. All this tension and stress you're feeling is never going to allow you to access old memories you've been hiding for years."

"I'm not hiding them. I can't help it. Do you honestly think I haven't tried?"

"Not at all. More than likely, your brain is protecting you. Whatever happened that night had to be painful. Probably more so than any one person should have to endure. Personally, I wish you could leave it alone and let it stay in the past where it belongs."

She pushed at his chest, still not budging him. "I've already done that for too long. I've been selfish enough. If something in my memory can help Savannah, then I owe that to my brother."

This time it was he who shook his head. "You don't owe anyone anything. You, Nina are a grown woman as is Savannah Lewis. She made a choice to come forward, something she did not have to do. Whatever demons she has that made her do that are not your responsibility."

"But don't you see? That's exactly why I need to talk to her. Why now? What changed after all these years? I mean, what are we missing?"

"Then tomorrow we'll go see her."

Nina rolled her eyes. "Told ya. I knew you would make a big production out of this instead of letting me handle it on my own."

"God, woman. You have no idea how badly I need to take you over my knee right now. In fact, I don't think I've ever met anyone who needs a spanking more than you do."

Nina's stomach jerked and a sudden pressure pulsed between her thighs at his vehement suggestion. She felt her eyes grow wide, but couldn't stop them.

Oh dear God. This time she pushed and shoved and wrestled her way out of his arms. *What the hell?* Or better yet, what the hell was wrong with her?

Something inside her had snapped and she wanted to do it.

Right here. Right now.

She wanted the devil himself to spank her.

CHAPTER SIX

*G*abe watched the myriad of emotions crossing Nina's face as he braced for her explosive reaction. What he'd suggested probably shocked her to her core, but seriously, this woman needed a firm hand.

His hand.

When he saw what looked like shame fill her features he'd had enough. He grabbed her by the hand and led her to his office.

"Gabe, what—?" she sputtered.

He remained quiet as he grappled with his self-control. Based on her reactions to his touches alone, he was fairly certain she would soon give consent to more. And he sure as hell wanted more. So much so that his cock had gone hard at the mere thought of her draped over his lap giving him access to her beautiful heart-shaped ass.

As much as he'd tried to keep to the straight and narrow with her in his house, he couldn't always keep his mind out of the gutter. Not when she looked at him with needy eyes, or when she clung to him in her sleep, or even when the tears dripped down her cheeks as she fought with her own demons of frustration.

But this...

This was an all new level of hell.

He could no longer stand idly by offering her support when something as simple as a spanking had caused her what he was almost certain had to be shame. That royally pissed him off.

He closed the door behind him, more for effect than necessity considering they were alone in the house and he expected no further interruptions today. It worked too, judging by the way she stared at the closed door with an uncertainty that again rocked him to his core.

"Don't do that." He came to an abrupt halt and pulled her into his arms.

"What?" she asked, finally turning toward his voice.

"Look at my door like you've lost your last

chance at freedom. You know me, Nina. I am not going to hurt you. At least, not until you ask me to. The choice to submit is, and always will be, your choice."

"What's that supposed to mean?" she asked.

He gripped her chin and pulled her attention where he wanted it—squarely on him. "Just what it sounded like, I suppose."

In that moment, he watched the fire return to her eyes and waited again for the outburst he expected. To his surprise, she clamped her mouth shut and crossed her arms over her chest, choosing to use her body to declare her obstinance.

"God, you are such a brat. Good thing I know how to deal with brats."

"Don't try to handle me like one of your Purgatory girls. I am not like that."

Guess she couldn't keep that mouth shut after all.

"No, Angel. You most certainly are not at all like the other women I know. You are one of a kind and you've been teaching me that lesson for more years than I care to count. Come here so we can talk." He took a seat on the brown leather couch he kept in his office solely because this was the kind of moment he'd been hoping for when he designed this room.

He had often imagined her in here, naked and waiting while he finished work. Or maybe sitting at his feet while he took a phone call with his fingers buried deep inside her as she tried to maintain her composure as to not alert the caller that she was about to come all over his hand...

He inwardly groaned. These fantasies were not helping. Although he filed both scenarios away and made plans to use them both on his little brat as soon as she was ready.

When she tried to take a seat next to him, he tugged on her arm until she fell in his lap.

"Gabe!" she squeaked, losing her balance and falling against his chest.

It felt good to have her settled against him. He would've preferred her naked, but they would have time for that later.

First things first.

"You could've warned me," she said, straightening her body and adjusting her shirt.

"Never count on that, darlin'. A Dom's favorite weapon is the element of surprise."

"Is that what we're doing? You are Domming me now?"

Gave allowed a small sigh to escape. "Don't try to analyze this. That's never going to work. I already know in here." He gently touched her chest with his fingertip. "That you trust me. So why don't you sit back, relax and listen. You're way too uptight."

She took a deep breath and slowly exhaled. "You're right, this has already been one hell of a day. And for that matter a month, the year, even a decade."

She settled against him, even laying her head on his chest. The soft, silky strands of her rich brown hair brushed against his neck, forcing him to hold his breath and count to ten. Every touch, every sigh and pretty much everything about her got to him. Always had. Always would.

"You always want to carry the weight of the world on your shoulders, never asking anyone for help. In that respect you're pretty much just like your brothers."

A slight snort/giggle erupted out of her, totally unbidden and one hundred percent all Nina. She wasn't the only one wound tight. They both needed this time.

"I'd never even heard of BDSM before college. We were from a small, conservative town in the middle of nowhere where the most exciting thing that happened was some redneck startin' trouble at the local Piggly Wiggly. But after the accident, when your brothers kind of adopted me, they took me everywhere they went. Including a sex club in Raleigh during my junior year. Ironically, they claimed *I* was too uptight and deemed that I needed to get laid. And thus my journey to becoming a dominant began."

He ran his fingers along her spine, up and down, and taking note of the slow ease of her muscles as she began to relax.

"Oh, I totally figured it was their fault. That's just the how. What about the why?"

"Take it easy, I'm getting there. Hasn't anyone ever told you that all good things come to those who wait?"

"That's just what people say when they're trying to avoid telling you the truth."

He laughed, it was hard not to. She had a comeback for everything. "You southern girls have no patience."

She giggled again. "Best remember that, huh?"

"Normally, that would earn you another spanking. Luckily for you, I'm not keeping track yet."

She lifted her head and looked at him, her eyes

slightly dilated. "You seem fixated on the spanking thing. I thought you didn't want to hurt me?"

"That's not what I said at all. Sometimes it takes a little pain before pleasure to get your head on straight. Then there are other times when pain can actually enhance pleasure."

"I don't know about that." She sighed. "Pain just sounds like pain. Although I'm not blind. I've watched many scenes at Purgatory where a sub was either being flogged, spanked or whipped that somehow led to an explosive orgasm. I just don't think that would work for me."

"Have you ever tried it?" He cringed inwardly at his question simply because if she said yes he really didn't want to know about it. The protectiveness he felt towards this woman often leaned towards the extreme. And the idea of another man touching her without his permission created a dark ball of anger that roiled in his stomach looking for escape.

She shook her head against his chest and some of the tension inside him eased.

"No," she whispered.

Of course the sick bastard he was, now wanted to know why the hell not? Like a fucking stalker he'd watched her at Purgatory from afar. But close enough that he saw her cheeks flush and her hands shake from watching those very scenes. There was no mistaking they aroused her.

"Because you're afraid?"

She stayed silent, specifically not answering his question. After a few minutes of quiet, Gabe threaded his fingers through her silky hair and tugged just enough on the strands to force her to lift her head and look at him.

"Answer the question, Nina. I think we've already established how important honesty and trust is in this situation."

"I believe there are some things better left unsaid. Some doors, once opened, can never be closed again. I can't risk that."

The sadness in her non-answer was unmistakable, so much so that he was left with an inexplicable ache in his chest. Nevertheless, he had to know what the hell she meant.

"You can't risk what exactly?" he questioned.

She looked back at him, the sadness now darkening her normally vibrant eyes. "Don't do this. You're asking me to risk our friendship. A friendship I'm not sure I could live without."

For half a second he thought he could let it go. Then her bottom lip quivered and a sheen of tears pooled in her eyes. He'd always had a weakness for making his subs cry. He viewed tears as the near ultimate act of vulnerability and intimacy. And had he mentioned he was a sick bastard? While tears could be cathartic in healing, they also made his dick hard. Not that he was suffering in that department.

"I'm not going anywhere and neither is our friendship. No matter what happens between us or what we might learn about each other, nothing can alter how much I care about you and specifically what happens to you. So stop letting fear hold you back. We all have to take risks. It's the only way to win big."

"That's easy for you to say. You don't have anything to lose."

"That's naïve of you to think so. Everyone everywhere always has something to gain or lose. Always. Now stop evading my question and tell me the real reason why you've never participated in a scene."

Anger flashed across her face, almost making him laugh with its predictability. Filled with a fervent passion for life, his Nina always ran hot or cold. She was not a lukewarm woman. Now it would be his job to temper some of her emotions and channel it into something far more productive and/or pleasurable.

Watching her suffer these last few weeks had been hard to bear. How many times had he considered yanking her under his control to stop it? The only thing that stopped him had been the serious nature of her repressed memories. They weren't to be taken lightly.

Several more minutes passed without her uttering a word and while he considered himself to be a patient man, he did have his limits.

"Nina," he warned.

"Fine," she huffed. "I never tried it because the right man never asked."

Some of Gabe's tension eased once she said the words, but the part of his body being fueled by arousal flared to life.

Fuck. This woman. She would be the death of him.

She hadn't said the exact words he'd been hoping for, but they were there just the same. She'd been waiting for him.

And he'd been an asshole and not pursued her. Primarily because Mason had demanded it. For some reason the lifestyle was good enough for all of them, but not good enough for her.

Or maybe all roads led back to the same fucking scenario. The night of their father's death. They all acted like they wanted her memories to return, but their actions didn't exactly match up on that.

By treating her with kid gloves and making sure she didn't get too involved in their lives, it kept her in that same limbo she'd lingered in for over a decade.

He'd definitely have to give some more thought to her brother's motivations, but not now. Right now he needed his focus solely on Nina.

"And who is the right man?" he asked. Yes, maybe his ego was starting to get the best of him, but that didn't change the fact he needed to hear her say it.

"Now you're just being a jerk."

He chuckled. "I've been called much worse. By you, many times. In fact, I'd dare say jerk is quite an improvement. Nevertheless, there is one thing that should be crystal clear in this negotiation."

"What's that?"

He gazed into her eyes, relieved that the sadness and anger that had previously filled them had given way to something else. Curiosity or resignation maybe?

"When we do this, and considering you're still here on my lap and not fighting me too badly, I'd bet we will be doing this, it will be because we both have agreed that it's something that we want. I am not coercing you into anything. In order for this to work, your consent is key."

"I'm aware," she replied, her voice lowering to a husky whisper that cracked at the end.

That noise raced along his skin and nearly punched him in the balls with the sheer force of its effect. With every passing moment he could feel a little more of his control slipping away.

Hell, he was a red-blooded male after all and he had the woman of his dreams sitting on his lap. So of course, all he could think about was getting inside her one way or another.

"Are you going to say it?" he asked.

She sighed, her breath coming out in a heated puff that brushed across his skin, eating away at more of his infamous control.

When it came to Nina, all bets seemed to be off. His rigid standards were all set to jump out the window and flee from the scene. This was not a good sign at all.

"You know the truth already. Why do I have to say it? It's too hard."

"And that's why it means so much to me. I've waited a really long time to hear it. I think we both deserve the truth."

She sighed again. "I don't see you laying your cards out on the table any more than I have."

Touché. Nina wasn't a pushover. Never had been and never would be.

He gently grasped her chin and tilted her head until their eyes met. "Nina, you're in my goddamned home. In my bed every night. Your scent is in every room of my house taunting me day and night. You know what I want. However, what I want isn't the priority at the moment. You are. So stop stalling and decide. You've had more than enough time to think this through."

CHAPTER SEVEN

Nina curled her fingers into Gabe's shirt and breathed deep. He wasn't the only one affected by proximity. Just because she wasn't sure how to handle him right now didn't mean she wasn't dying for more.

"It wasn't supposed to be like this, you know."

His fingers tightened at her waist where'd he'd been caressing her for the last ten minutes. "Then tell me how you think it was supposed to be," he demanded, his tone a little harsher than before.

Her stomach flipped, as it always did when he spoke to her like that. Her brain balked, reminding her that she wasn't supposed to get excited when a man demanded anything from her.

Inwardly she cringed. This-this thing she'd

inherited from her father worried her almost constantly. If she gave in, would she become like him? Would her intense desires turn dark and twisted like his?

Those thoughts made her want to cut and run. This war between the bad and the good inside her kept her constantly on edge and at this point, she just wanted it to stop. Any way she could make it happen.

"I wanted to be good," she whispered. "Not sick like him."

Gabe jerked underneath her. "What did you say?"

His tone had lowered, sounding darker. It made gooseflesh rise along the back of her neck.

"My father," she whispered. "As far as I can tell everything bad about him had something to do with sex."

The moment the words left her mouth, Gabe's entire body went rigid.

"And you think I'm like him."

His response wasn't a question and it shocked her. "God no! It's not you at all I'm worried about. It's me. I have that bastard's blood running through my veins. That most likely means whatever darkness was in him is likely in me, too." That usually well buried feeling of shame rushed forward again, reminding her why she usually avoided these kind of confrontations. Gabe knew a lot about her family, but she doubted he knew the true depths of her father's depravity. Hell, she likely didn't know it all either.

Gabe remained silent, allowing the fear and tension inside her to grow. She only half wanted to know what he must be thinking. She studied him for clues. His eyes said nothing, but his darkening complexion along with the clenching and unclenching of his jaw said enough. In fact, he kind of looked like he was about to explode.

"That's bullshit, Nina. You are not like him. None of you are. Fuck, what is wrong with people these days? Being into kink and control doesn't make you some sort of sick criminal. That's all in your head. Jesus." He lifted his hands and shoved his fingers in his hair, pulling on the strands until they nearly stood on end.

"Who the hell put those thoughts in your head?"

She shrugged, not wanting to admit the truth. Maybe her mother had made a few suggestions back in the day, but it wasn't all her fault. Nina had let those thoughts fester in her mind for a very long time, allowing them to become her greatest fears.

"You're a grown ass woman, Nina Fairchild. You know damn well that sex is not some evil entity that made your father do the things he did. That was his mind. He was sick. Wait." He wrapped his arms around her and pressed his forehead to hers. "Did he-?"

Nina nearly choked at the unspoken question. How many times had she asked herself that same question? The sad part was she didn't know the answer. Not really. First, she had to...

"Nina." He gently grasped her chin again and moved her head until their gazes met again. "I need you here with me, baby, not in your head. This is important."

"I know," she gasped as panic inside her rose. "I just don't know what to tell you."

"The truth. Always. Whatever it is we'll deal with it together."

"Why?"

His forehead wrinkled in confusion. "Why, what? Why do I need the truth? We've already been over that. I can't help you if you can't be honest."

She furiously shook her head. "No. That's not

what I meant," She took a deep breath and exhaled slowly before she continued. She was walking onto dangerous ground now and she knew it. "Why are we going to deal with it together? Why are you subjecting yourself to this drama? You don't have to do this. I mean, it's not fair to you."

Gabe reared back, an unreadable look on his face. She held her breath.

"What the fuck, Nina? What the hell kind of question is that?"

Her whole body began to tremble. "I know we're kinda sorta family in a way, but what you're taking on with me is way more than is called for."

In a way, it sickened her to burden him, of all people, with her problems. He certainly didn't deserve having to clean up this mess. Hence, why she wanted to go and talk to Savannah on her own and figure this crap out.

His eyes narrowed slightly and she swore his dark eyes got darker as anger flared across his face.

"That's fucking bullshit. I'm here now and I've been here every time you have needed me because- You. Are. Mine. I may not be your lover, *yet*, but I'm not one of your brothers either. So get that out of your head right now."

She sucked in a sharp breath as he moved his

face closer to hers, her mind reeling. "But you are mine, nonetheless. And you have been for a very long time. Obviously I waited way too long to make that crystal clear right here." He tapped the side of her head. "In fact, this isn't working." He lifted her off his lap and deposited her on the leather couch.

Immediately, she missed his touch. She might have let out a strangled cry to confirm that. Nonetheless, he stood and crossed the room. He opened one of the cabinets behind his desk and pulled out something she couldn't see. He then returned to the couch and crouched down in front of her.

Now she could tell that he had some sort of roll that looked like it was made out of velvet. She scrunched her forehead. What the hell? He unrolled what ended up looking like nothing more than a thin piece of padding and placed it on the floor in front of where she sat.

He then stood and took several steps back.

"On your knees, Nina."

Taken aback by his sudden request, she went stock-still. Her mind reeled at the sudden turn of events.

"Excuse me?" she said.

"I said, on your knees. I didn't ask for your questions or invite you to say anything further. You will do as I request, answer all of my questions truthfully and in return I will give you whatever you need."

Nina blinked at the harsh tone of his words. They shocked her to hear them after all this time. Yet, somewhere deep inside her, they connected. So much so, that a huge part of her was already aching to just do it already.

Seconds ticked by as she remained frozen in her indecision. Gabe said nothing more. He only stared down at her, practically daring her to do it. At least, that was how she chose to interpret the hard look in his eyes.

Her body softened with desire. How many times had she dreamed of this exact scenario? In those dreams, her braver self gave herself over to this man time and time again and she loved every second of it.

So what was holding her back now?

Fear, she wanted to cry out.

This was the one aspect of her life she'd been unable to face thus far, despite all of her bravado and success in other ways. Move out on her own? Check. Start her own business? Check. Develop friendships and have some fun? Check. Meet a man and enjoy a healthy sex life? Uhhh...

With all of those thoughts running wild through her head, Nina had not realized she'd moved from the couch. At least, not until her knees caressed the soft velvet padding underneath them.

She inhaled sharply at the realization she'd done it. Oh. My. God.

"Jesus Christ, you're beautiful on your knees."

Her head shot up at the reverent tone from Gabe. He seemed just as surprised as she felt. She swallowed thickly around the lump in her throat and closed her eyes, letting the moment wash over her.

She felt Gabe move closer as the air around her was displaced. She sighed when his fingers stroked down her cheek and she leaned her face into his hand.

"Baby, you really have no idea how precious you are to me. This moment is a beautiful gift that I am never going to forget."

Her pulse quickened as she listened to the calming tone of his voice. She thought she'd had an idea of what she meant to him, but then he said she was his. And then there was that word *yet* when he talked about being her lover.

They weren't lovers, *yet*. Her stomach jolted.

"Nina, open your eyes. Talk to me. I need you to answer my question. This is important."

She opened her eyes, blinking in surprise to discover Gabe crouched beside her, his face only inches away from hers.

"What question?" she asked.

"Your father, Nina. Was he ever inappropriate with you? Sexually, I mean."

Nina felt a keening cry in her head and she squeezed her eyes shut against it. At least she hoped it was only in her head. She didn't want to think about him right now. Not when she felt this vulnerable--this open.

"I—I don't think so. Unless..." She couldn't bear thinking about it, let alone saying it.

"Unless what?" he asked.

Of course Gabe would push. He always would. Wasn't that what he'd told her? He wanted her to get her memories back so she could move forward with her life. And in his opinion that meant facing the past.

She shook her head, trying to refuse those thoughts from going any further. They were too hard to talk about.

"It's okay, Nina. You're safe. Always safe with me. Do you understand?"

She nodded, still not wanting to say anymore.

"The word unless refers to the one night you don't remember, right? You think he might have done something to you then?"

"I don't know. Maybe. God, don't you think I've tried to remember? That stupid blank spot in my memory is driving me slowly crazy." She tried to control the whine in her voice to no avail. "I'm so tired of this. This not knowing is too much."

"Shhh." Gabe leaned forward and pressed his lips to her forehead and she savored the touch, as she always did.

The man had a knack for calming her down whenever she needed it. Shame welled inside her. She'd been using Gabe as her crutch for weeks and what had he gotten in return? A headache maybe.

"I'm sorry," she whispered. "You've got to be tired of all of my non answers by now."

He chuckled. "I've always enjoyed a challenge. And besides, I did get you on your knees for me. That's progress."

A small smile crept across her face. "You're a hard man to say no to."

This time he snorted. "Babe, you've been saying it just fine for years now."

She lifted her head so she could look at him. As

always, he looked down at her as if he could see straight through her. "I don't want to say no anymore. I've never *wanted* to say no. I just didn't know how to say yes. I still don't."

Gabe said nothing. He simply leaned forward and captured her lips with his. Heat speared through her as the simple slide of his tongue prodded her to open for more. She did.

He delved inside and her world titled on its axis. Desire rushed forward as he grabbed her face and took them both even deeper. She moaned into his mouth, her mind and body aching for so much more. She always wanted more from him.

Their tongues tangled, with his dominant in its exploration. Her mind reeled as she locked away all the reasons she couldn't do this with him. Nothing mattered except him. Gabe. The man she loved.

She dug deep for the strength to shove her fear away and simply revel in the feelings of arousal and hard shockwaves of need now rushing over her as both their need threatened to overwhelm her.

But it wasn't just the fact their mouths were fused in an out of this world kiss that had Nina reeling. Nope. His hands were at work too.

From her arms to her waist, there wasn't an

inch he hadn't caressed. The fact he'd found her nipples hiding behind two layers of clothing did nothing to lessen the sensations that shot through her every time he flicked one or the other.

She groaned, unable to hold back her reactions. There were too many things happening at once for her to squash any of the zings of pleasure that continued to sizzle through her long after he moved on to another spot.

Everything felt so incredible she started plotting how to get out of her clothes without breaking contact. If his touch got her going this hot and this fast, her whole body might explode if they were skin to skin. Something that didn't sound all together horrible at the moment.

All too soon, and right after she began to squirm, Gabe broke their kiss and stared down at her. His finger stroked her bottom lip.

"I lied to you this morning," he said.

"How?" she said, the word barely a whisper with adrenalin coursing through her.

"I told you we could do this without sex. I lied. I can't touch you and not want more. That's clear now and you should know that going in. Hell, from one kiss I'm barely able to stop myself from ripping your clothes off so I can get all the way inside you.

And even if I could keep my dick in my pants, I can't stop myself from thinking about what you taste like. And not just your mouth, baby. I want to taste all of you, especially your pussy when you come for me."

"Gabe," she gasped. She could hardly believe the words he'd just said, let alone grasp the way her body responded to them. Her skin was on fire now and she needed him to do something to relieve the burn.

"And that's exactly why I had to tell you the truth now. I can't watch you open like a flower for me and then do nothing about it. The more we progress, the more you'll need to come and I'm not about to leave you like that forever. Hell, you'll beg me to come and I sure as hell won't say no."

Her mind short-circuited. He had to stop talking about making her come or she was going to be in a puddle on the floor any minute. And she highly doubted what he'd just started would be relieved by her normal tools of the trade.

No, her hand and the occasional toy were certainly not going to cut it this time.

"I'm scared," she admitted, albeit reluctantly.

"I know you are and rightfully so. When I get in the zone, I can and will come on strong.

Normally that response is tightly controlled, but when it comes to you I'm not one hundred percent sure how I will react." He leaned forward and touched his forehead to hers. "But I know I'd never hurt you. At least not in a way that you didn't find pleasurable."

As if to emphasize his point, he reached up and pinched both her nipples in a shockingly hard and steady grip.

She gasped, shocked at the pain, but even more so at how that sensation seemed to be connected in a direct path to her clit. When she bucked her hips and for a moment believed he was about to make her come that easy, he released her.

"No!" she whined.

A dark chuckle filled the room as he lifted his head away from her. "See what I mean? Another few seconds and you'd ask to come."

Nina closed her eyes and tried to find the words to deny it. Just because he was right didn't mean she wanted to admit it. At this point, Gabe's confidence knew no bounds. He certainly didn't need any encouragement from her.

A few minutes later, when she finally got some of the desire raging through her under a semblance of control, her brain kicked in. Along with a healthy dose of anxiety.

She lifted her lashes and stared into Gabe's eyes. It would be so easy to go along with him and get lost in everything he offered. She didn't doubt that for however long it lasted, it would be amazing. There wasn't anything he couldn't do.

But he'd asked for her complete honesty...

"There's something I should probably tell you." She hesitated and dropped her face into her hands. God this was going to be so embarrassing.

He grabbed her hands and pulled them away from her face. "Look at me," he said.

Slowly, she lifted her head and faced him again.

"Whatever it is, it's going to be fine. Nothing you tell me will ever leave this room unless you decide to divulge it. Seriously, Nina. I swear to you that your secrets will be my secrets for as long as we live. I will never betray you. And definitely no judgment. I have not lived a perfect life and I'd never expect someone else to. We've all had our fair share of mistakes."

Based on his words she could tell his mind had gone down the wrong path. Although she catalogued his comment about his own life for further examination. She'd love to get in on some of his secrets.

"It's not what you're thinking. I really can't remember anything that happened that last night with the reverend. I'm not lying about that."

He squeezed her arms a little tighter. "I didn't think you did. I only meant whatever you have to say is okay. It's important to me that you trust me and that means with anything. My word is my bond. I don't break it."

She shook her head. He still had no idea. Her only fear of telling him her secret meant that it would change what kind of relationship he wanted from her. A sexy, virile man like him with obviously intense needs wasn't the type of guy to be put off indefinitely.

Before she could spit it out, he leaned forward and captured her lips again. This time with the sweetest, softest kiss she could ever have imagined. Unlike the urgent, need fueled kiss from before, this time he moved slow, as if he not only had all the time in the world, but he wanted to use all of it solely for her.

A soft sigh formed in her throat. Her chest tightened as her mind began to melt under this new kind of onslaught.

Nina jerked away. "Wait. We have to stop or I'm never going to get this out."

He nodded, a slight smile teasing her from the edge of his mouth.

"Then tell me."

She took one last breath and then blurted it out in one constant string of words without stopping. "I can't have sex with you. I mean as much as I want to, and I really really want to. I don't think that's ever been the question. I mean, get real. You look like the devil and you kiss like one too. If ever there was a man to sin with it would be you. But I made a pact with my mother, and before you say anything, I know. She's more than a little touched. And almost as religiously obsessed as my father was. Yet, I made a promise and I've held onto that promise as the one good thing that came out of my childhood. Other than Tucker that is. Because he was always so good to me and was the best big brother a girl could hope for—"

Before she could finish, Gabe covered her mouth with his hand. "Take a breath, baby. You're talking so fast I can barely understand a word of it."

Nina shook her head and tried grabbing his hand.

"Nope. Deep breath first. You need to calm down. Then you can tell me more."

She could see the sheer determination in the hard set of his jaw and by the tone of his voice that he wasn't going to let her finish unless she did as he asked. So she took a deep breath through her nose and then exhaled even slower, being sure to roll her eyes at him through the whole process.

"You do realize every time you do that it only makes me want to pull you over my knee even more, right? I mean my dick's hard enough, baby. Don't make it worse."

This time she slapped at his hand until he finally released her. "I can't believe you aren't taking me seriously. I was trying to be honest with you like you asked."

His smile died. "And I appreciate your honesty. But you were on the verge of turning blue. How about we cut to the chase then? What pact did you make with your mother that prevents you from having sex with me?"

Blood rushed to Nina's cheeks with his more blunt than usual questions. However, his ego and his need for control gave her plenty of confidence to take some of the wind out of his sails.

"It's not about you. It's me. I made an old-fashioned pact with my mother that I would not have sex until I got married. And believe it or not, I have kept my word. Not that it's always been easy, mind you. I was a stupid kid back then who had no idea what she was getting into, but nonetheless, I did it. As much as it sucks, I'm not sure I can break it now. There are already too many broken things in my life. If at all possible, I'd like to do one thing right and this might be all I've got left to make that a reality."

CHAPTER EIGHT

*G*abe felt his world tilt on its axis more than he saw it. Blood rushed through his ears making it impossible to hear anything else Nina said. Had she really just confessed to being a virgin?

How was that even possible? Shy, introverted girls were the ones to watch out for. Not the outspoken, vibrant and slightly wild ones like his Nina. They were NOT virgins.

A fucking pact? Really?

"Fuck me," he said without even thinking.

She scrunched up her mouth a moment before she responded. "Did you not hear a word I said? I just told you I can't. I mean we really can't."

It was his turn to shake his head. "Jesus, Nina. I didn't mean that literally. Well, I did but—fuck. No, I didn't. Fuck! You're a virgin?"

He didn't mean to raise his voice, but she had said the very last thing he would have ever imagined that would come out of her mouth and blown his mind.

She picked herself up from her knees and glared down at him. "You don't have to yell it like it's some kind of dirty word or worse, the plague. Fuck you, okay? Just fuck you."

She started past him and he barely used his brain before he grabbed her arm and stopped her.

"Marry me," he blurted.

She whirled on him, a combination of disbelief and anger stamped across her face. That didn't bode well for him so he braced for impact.

"Excuse me? Did you seriously just *tell* me to marry you? Are you high?"

In that moment his rash words crystallized in his mind. They weren't a joke. In fact, he'd never been more serious in his life than right here in this moment. It was the perfect solution to more than one of their problems.

"No, I am *not* high. I am in fact, quite serious."

She shook her head. "Well, then I must have missed the part where you hit your head and have a concussion then. Because, you know, who the hell wants to get married just so they can have sex?" She threw her hand up and slapped it against her head. "Oh yeah. Crazy people and now, I guess, you."

Gabe rose to his full height and scowled down at the woman he wanted to marry.

Marry.

He rolled the word around in his mind for a moment to see how it felt. And like his gut had suggested minutes ago, it felt right.

"What exactly is so crazy about getting married? You admitted not fifteen minutes ago that you've been waiting for me."

"I did no—"

"Don't," he warned, his voice low and gravelly now as he felt that need again to take her over his knee and spank her until she confessed everything to him through a stream of hard fought tears. "Don't deny what you've already said. We promised the truth, remember?"

She clamped her lips shut and flared her nostrils.

"Enough already. You're starting to sound like a

broken record, Gabe Michaels. This is too much even for you. You manage the largest sex club in three states, you can have your pick of any woman you desire and they don't need you to marry them first. Go choose one of them to take care of your needs."

He took a deep breath to calm the fire burning in his chest from her carelessly chosen words. "First, I'm not sure I want to know how you know Purgatory is the largest sex club in the tri-state area. And second, I don't want them. I want you. Maybe I've been waiting for you, too. You ever think of that?"

That got her opening and closing her mouth several times without saying a word. Finally, the woman was speechless. Intent on taking advantage of her silence, he continued, "I know you think we're just friends and that's more important than everything else. But don't you see? That's exactly what makes this so perfect.

We already know each other and have for a very long time. I think that's more than a lot of newlyweds can say these days. It's not like we're one of those people who are going to wake up after a night of drinking in Las Vegas and find themselves hitched to a total stranger. We're smarter than that."

"Not sure I'd choose smarter as the right word."

Gabe bit back a grin. Did she realize she'd just implied she was actually thinking about his proposal?

He had to admit, if only to himself, the idea had been an impulsive one. But the more he thought about it, the more he liked it. Nina needed his protection and care, and as her husband that would be a hell of a lot easier.

Maybe he couldn't lock her up in a gilded prison to keep her out of harm's way, but he could certainly use his charm and influence to keep predators away. Especially if she ended up having anything to do with her father's murder all those years ago.

A fact he still couldn't wrap his mind around.

Yes, she was hot-headed and stubborn and could have an emotional outburst when provoked, but that hardly made her a killer. Either that bastard had done something unspeakable to her or her brothers were dead wrong about what happened.

Either way, he wasn't about to let anything happen to Nina. He had no problem lying or cheating to keep her safe or to capture her heart, for that matter. He just knew he was done waiting.

"I beg to differ. This might be the smartest idea I've ever had." He looked over at the antique clock hanging on the wall and smiled. "If we hurry we should be able to get down to the courthouse and get this done today."

Nina choked. "What?!"

Her eyes had grown wide and her face was definitely flushed red. Of course that made him think of her skin that similar shade of color from either arousal or the sting of his whip. As soon as they got this done, they were going to try a scene with his favorite tool. The sooner he got her to let down her guard and into subspace the sooner they could work past some of her issues.

"I didn't really picture you as the kind of woman who wanted the whole big ceremony thing. Of course, if you'd prefer to wait and plan a wedding, we could hire someone to pull something together quickly. Whatever you'd like, as long as we handle this soon," he said.

"I'd like for you to stop talking about our marriage now as if it were already a done deal. This is insane. We have no business getting married."

Again, he noticed she hadn't said no. He'd shocked her, but underneath the bluster and pissy attitude he could see the woman who wanted to consider his offer.

"That argument isn't going to work. We've both already admitted that our interest in each other has deep roots. However, if that's not enough there is the logical reasoning that as your husband, I can legally be your confidant without risk in a court of law should I withhold information. I can help you explore the truth of your past and you'll be safe in every way."

She sucked in a sudden gasp of air and he immediately knew he'd hit the wrong chord with that nugget.

"You're an asshole," she said. "And a liar. All that lip service about believing I didn't kill my own father. You do think I did it. Just like them. Always like them. I should have known you would be on their side. You always are."

Gabe tightened his grip on Nina's arm. He was learning quickly that his unending patience with others didn't quite fully extend to his future bride. Listening to her hurl unfounded insults at him hurt more than it should.

"I think you should stop before you go too far."

He kept his voice low and his words measured in an attempt to keep his emotions in check. Whatever feelings this woman provoked in him, he wasn't sure either of them were truly ready to deal with them.

"I'm not your submissive, Gabe. I don't have to obey."

The way her voice cracked on the last word gave her farce away. That and the thousand other little signs she'd given him over the years. While it was true that Nina was an independent, strong-willed, stand on her own two feet kind of woman, it wasn't everything. She had layers and facets she'd yet to reveal other than in glimpses. He knew, because he paid attention to everything.

In his job and his life, he focused on the details. They were everything to him. And from his experience, he already knew that everyone gave away insights about themselves without ever realizing it.

"But you want to be." He narrowed his eyes and shook his head when she started to speak. "Don't waste your breath. Actions always speak louder than words, babe, and your actions and reactions say something totally different than your mouth. So instead of following some ideal you have in your brain, why don't you try listening to your heart?

Stop fighting and give yourself a chance to be whatever it is *you* want to be. For once in your life, stop worrying about what everyone else thinks and give something to yourself."

Several seconds ticked by with neither of them saying anything else as he let his words sink in. Gabe dug deep to find a little extra patience so he could give her the time she needed right now to think this through.

"That's not as easy as you think. I may have the weirdest family on the planet, but we're very connected. What they think matters."

Gabe's chest loosened. This woman gave so much for her family. It was past time someone gave back to her. "You deserve to be cared for as much as they do. Look around you. They've all found a way to carve out some happiness in the midst of the chaos. You can too. Marry me and I will do everything in my power to help you. We can talk to Savannah together. If that doesn't work, we'll try something else. If you hear nothing else I've said, hear this. I will do anything, and I literally mean anything, to make you happy. Will I demand we do things my way? Hell yes. I thrive on control. Especially when obedience is given freely. The crux however, is about pleasure and happiness. It would be my goal in life to give you everything your heart desires in a way that suits us both. It's not wrong to be a submissive. Especially not when you have a Dom who desires nothing more than to provide for anything that you need. I don't want to change you, baby. I want you to be free."

CHAPTER NINE

Nina sat silently in the back seat of Gabe's town car as his driver rushed her to the courthouse after a quick stop at her house to change into something more marriage appropriate and to pack. Not only were they supposedly getting married, but apparently, they were going on a secret honeymoon for the weekend as well.

She could still hardly believe that she'd said yes to this insanity. Maybe it had been a moment of weakness. Maybe not. The constant fluttering of her stomach made her uneasy. Was it due to excitement or fear?

This was Gabe. The man she'd counted on forever. The friend she'd dreamed about having benefits with. She dropped her gaze from the passing scenery to the hands she had clenched in her lap. These last few weeks had turned her world upside down and that was clearly saying something considering how weird her life had always been.

Devout religious mother who had a thing for the extreme. An absentee father who had turned out to be an egotistical serial polygamist and a preacher, too. Then there were the half siblings coming out of the woodwork. Not that she had any real numbers on that. Her brother Mason had a stubborn streak about keeping family information under wraps. That included keeping her somewhat in the dark.

Then there was the sudden confession of Savannah Lewis to the murder of her husband and Nina's father, Reverend Lewis. No matter how hard she tried to distract herself, it all went back to Savannah and that night.

Gah! She was so tired of going round and round about this in her head. This persistent memory block had taken enough of her life. Now she had a decision to make. Go through with this farce of a marriage. Let Gabe provide her the protection she needed to truly explore her mind while submitting to his control—or not.

Of course there was a lot more at stake than that. There was the matter of her heart and whether she could save it from being irreparably broken while allowing him to invade her life and her body.

Nina sighed. Why did she make a stupid pact with her mother and why after everything she'd been through, did she feel the need to honor it? That point burned inside her. She'd used that lame excuse as her crutch since—well, for more years than she cared to count.

It made it easy to keep her life in a forward moving progression without letting anyone get too close. In a weird way it had given her the freedom to observe Gabe in his natural environment without any pressure to do anything more.

What she'd learned over the years was that Gabe Michaels could be as ruthless as he was giving. He gladly helped anyone who needed it, but always on his terms. A pushover he was not.

As the car pulled into the parking garage attached to the county courthouse, the butterflies in her stomach grew frantic. The time for her final decision grew near and she didn't know what to do.

Part of her believed every word Gabe promised. She had no doubt he would do anything and everything to protect her from not only anyone who might come after her, but from herself.

And she certainly had no doubts that Gabe could and would follow through on his sexual promises as well. She had a feeling he would fulfill every dream she ever had and some she hadn't even thought of yet.

The moment the car came to a full stop, the rear door across from her opened and Gabe slid inside next to her as the driver exited the vehicle.

Nina clutched her chest. "Jesus, you scared the hell out of me."

He grinned over at her. "Who else were you expecting?"

"I wasn't expecting anyone. I just thought we were meeting inside."

Gabe leaned forward and pressed a soft kiss to her lips. "Not yet. We've got one more thing to deal with before we get married."

He handed her a slim manila folder. "What is it?" she asked.

"Prenup agreement."

She looked up at him, her eyes widening. "You think I'm going to try and steal your money? That's a little insulting at this point, don't you think? Not to mention a shitty way to prove you don't trust me after all. So much for all that talk back at your house."

Gabe laid the folder on her lap. "Babe, slow down. This prenup is for you not me. You want half of what I have if this doesn't work out? Done. That's how confident I am that this isn't going to be as temporary as you think. You are far more important than money to me. But you, babe, if we don't sign this and protect your assets, your brothers will kick my ass with Mason leading the charge."

She was pretty sure her mouth was hanging open but she didn't care. She was so stunned he'd gone to this length to protect *her* interests. He could have knocked her over with a feather.

She shook her head and closed her mouth, trying to clear her thoughts. "This was sweet and all, but I don't imagine you wanting anything to do with my cafe or the little cottage I own. You've got a lot more to lose than I do." At least when it came to financial assets, anyway. Unfortunately, there was no paperwork that could protect her heart in this situation. When she walked away from this deal with a broken heart that would have to be on her. She wasn't exactly going in on this blind.

"Nina, you are not that naive. Mason likes to keep things close to the vest, but even I know that you are worth a substantial amount of money. And none of your brothers would disagree with me on this. Your assets have to be protected from *anyone*."

For a second she had no idea what the hell he referred to before the rest of her brain kicked in. Her father's dirty money...

"I could care less about the money I got from my father's estate. If *you* want that, you can have it. I'll sign it over to you right now. I've told Mason a million times and I will tell you the same thing. I am never touching it. *Never*," she emphasized.

"That's the point of this," he held up the folder. "Whether you touch it or not matters little in the grand scheme of this plan. But it is there and I'm going to make damn sure it's protected—even from me."

"This is stupid. We're arguing over dirty money. This is going to ruin everything."

He shook his head. "Nope. All you have to do is sign this and it's all forgotten. I'll have this messengered over to my lawyer's office and he can deliver it to Mason for safekeeping."

Her eyes went wide. "Oh my God, wait. Isn't Victor your attorney? Holy shit. You told him we were getting married?" She glanced around the car looking through the windows for her nosy brother.

"He's probably already told Mason everything, who is going to show up here any minute."

"Victor is more of a professional than that."

"Victor is a jerk. He'll do whatever Mason tells him to."

Gabe's chuckle surrounded her. "He may come across as a hardass and a tool for your brother, which he often is, but he won't break his client confidentiality rules. Trust me."

She exhaled the breath she'd been holding. Every time she thought this situation would spiral out of control, Gabe had an answer. He'd apparently thought of everything.

He grabbed her hand. "Relax, Angel. I've got your back in this. You focus on relaxing your mind and enjoying the process ahead of you and I'll make sure the details are taken care of. That's my job." He slid the folder into her lap and handed her a pen.

She frowned. That felt a little one-sided. Wouldn't it be her job to take care of him? She stared down at the legal forms awaiting her signature. Funny how her immediate assumption had been him trying to protect himself from her when in actuality he'd done the opposite.

"I don't understand these lengths you are going to for all this. This isn't necessary."

"I already told you. Protecting you and your interests is what I do. I'll be responsible for your welfare and your happiness. So this is just the first of many things I plan to accomplish."

Nina bristled at his words. The Dom was broadcasting loud and clear. "You can't just take over my life. I'm perfectly capable of taking care of my own issues."

His right brow rose at her words and she practically felt the disapproval rolling off of him.

"No one said you weren't capable. However, you allowing me to take charge so you can focus on other things is a beautiful gift."

"Other things? As in sex?" She groaned.

He smirked down at her. "Do you want me to lie? I'm very invested in becoming your first. Do you have any idea what that means to a man like me?"

She shook her head. Honestly, she couldn't fathom what went through his head at this point.

"It means all I can think about is how no one else has been inside what's mine. Hell, I'm barely holding it together imagining how tight your sweet cunt is going to be when I finally get balls deep. It's going to be intense."

Nina swallowed at the rampant images his words put in her head. Sometimes it took his blunt words to remind her she wasn't dealing with an ordinary man. He had that extra dose of alpha possessiveness and the confidence that came with it that made her itch for more as much as it drove her crazy.

But maybe he was overestimating how great this would be. He didn't quite have the whole story. Time to confess the truth.

"I'm not exactly a virgin in the truest sense of the word, Gabe. I mean there's not much innocence in me, that's for sure. Over the years I have gotten creative to get around the actual insert dick part." She took a deep breath before she continued and averted her eyes. Not because she was ashamed, but simply because it was kind of hard to openly talk about this stuff. She didn't even share this much with her girlfriends. "For one, there's oral sex. I figured that didn't apply so I think I've perfected those skills." She bit her lips to keep from laughing when she watched his eyebrows raise from the corner of her eye. "And my toy closet is fairly extensive. I mean, it had to be though, because those nights I've spent watching at Purgatory tend to rev me up and I'm a normal woman with normal needs. Not to mention, I have a fairly vivid imagination. So I guess I'm just trying to let you know that..." She let the sentence trail off. Apparently, there was a limit as to how much she wanted to admit out loud.

"Your body already knows how to take a cock?"

Her body jerked at his question. "I guess if you want to put it that way then sure, yes."

"And you think taking my cock is going to be anything like one of your fake ones?"

She shrugged. "I'm sure it won't be exactly the same. I just didn't want you going into this thinking that—I don't know—that you'd hurt me or anything."

Gabe smiled a moment before he shoved the folder of papers to the floorboard of the car. "Lie back and lift your skirt, Nina."

"What?" With the blood now rushing through her ears at his sudden demand she couldn't be sure if she'd heard him right.

He sighed. "Babe, you just told me that you give good head and that you like to play with toys. Look at what that did?" He gestured to his lap. "So be a good girl and lie back and lift your skirt. You

need a preview of what's to come and I need a little
pussy time before we go in there."

"Just like that?" Thankfully, she managed to
keep the sudden fear out of her voice. Not that him
seeing her bare like that exactly scared her. Unless
she counted that it would probably be scary good.

"Yeah, babe. Just like that. Now don't make me
ask you again or our first order of business after the
ceremony will be a spanking."

A jolt of heat pulsed between her legs at what
was probably not an empty threat. *Oh God.* Was
she supposed to feel like that over the thought of
him bending her over his knee for discipline? What
was wrong with her?

With her pulse beating a wild staccato through
her body, she shifted sideways in the seat and lifted
her skirt while keeping her legs clenched together.

One of his eyebrows climbed up his forehead at
the same time a slight frown formed between his
pursed lips. *Oh God.* He was really going to do this.

Instead of telling her what he wanted her to do
this time, he simply grasped one of her ankles and a
knee and spread her wide.

A heated blush crawled up her body as she
imagined the wet spot he could now see on her
panties.

"Mmm," he hummed in obvious pleasure. "I can see nothing I've said so far has actually offended you. You're as wet for me as I am hard for you, aren't you?" He didn't wait for an answer as his fingers slid along her inner thigh and underneath the scrap of lace keeping her somewhat hidden.

As he dipped into her core, his eyes slid shut for a moment before opening again. His pupils were dilated now, making his eyes darker and more intense than ever.

"I'm glad you've learned to enjoy your toys, sweet girl, but rest assured when I sink into this heat it's going to feel nothing like your silicone versions. And just so you know, I do plan to ruin you for anyone else. No one is going to eat this sweet pussy like I will, nor will anyone ever fuck it endlessly like I plan to. Because this, Nina, is all mine."

Before she could begin to formulate a response, he withdrew his fingers, leaving her adrift just when it was getting good. He didn't make her wait long for what came next. He grabbed the edge of her delicate lace panties and ripped them apart.

"Hey! I liked those," she complained.

"You won't need them. I don't like barriers between me and my pussy."

Another jolt of excitement whipped through her. God, she was pretty damn sure she wasn't supposed to get so excited over a man being this possessive over her body, but someone needed to tell her body that. Because every time he did anything that had to do with him claiming her, it made her hotter.

Not that he gave her time to protest anyway. He immediately readjusted his position, leaning down between her thighs and began to feast.

Oh shit!

The little jolts of pleasure until now had been nothing compared to what happened the first time his tongue hit her tender flesh. This was a flat out detonation to her senses.

Apparently determined to use all of his tools at hand, Gabe devoured her with teeth, lips and tongue. Pleasure speared through her, making her buck her hips and lean forward in a desperate attempt for more. He chuckled against her for a moment before he lifted further away.

"Normally, I wouldn't let you come this early in the game, but since I want to walk in there and get married with the taste of your pleasure on my tongue there is no need to hold back."

Her skin caught fire on his words as her head

fell back on a moan. She couldn't stop anything if she tried. Especially not when he slid a finger inside her without warning.

"Look at me, sweet girl," he commanded. "I want you to watch everything I do, is that understood?"

By now, he was thrusting his finger in and out of her and she couldn't form words. Instead, she shook her head. Thankfully, he didn't push for more before he lowered his mouth to the one spot guaranteed to set her off.

With their gazes locked on each other, Nina's breath caught in her throat, the wave of an orgasm that promised to be epic began to build faster than she could process.

An onslaught of emotions she definitely couldn't cope with hovered at the edge of her mind until his teeth nipped at her clit and the new rush of sensation made everything else fall away.

Her muscles clenched and a low groan from Gabe vibrated across her sensitized skin, pushing her completely from the precipice she hovered. The scream that erupted from deep inside her was almost as intense as the orgasm Gabe had ripped from her in record time.

At some point in the process she'd closed her

eyes and by the time she recovered enough to open them, Gabe had moved closer, his face only inches from hers. His fingers however, were still sliding in and out of her in a slow steady rhythm.

"I knew you weren't a prude, but this kind of response is more than I'd even hoped for." He leaned forward and nipped at her inner thighs until she yelped.

"Gabe," she shrieked. "Are you trying to kill me?" She wiggled her butt in an attempt to lessen the friction, but in the back of his fancy car there was nowhere to escape the agonizing sensation of him working her over-sensitized lady bits.

"I am toying with the idea of making you come again."

"No way," she cried. "Too sensitive."

The smile that crept across his face came across as way too wicked for her comfort. She got the impression that Gabe would do whatever he wanted and she'd happily go along for the ride.

"Sure you can."

As if to punctuate his words, he curved his fingers and rubbed across her G-spot. Nina whimpered as her eyes rolled to the back of her head.

"I could make you come all day if I wanted. Over and over until you passed out from pleasure."

"I—I can't decide if that sounds good or evil." Already she could feel another wave building inside her. It seemed impossible to contemplate another release this soon, but apparently, Gabe was just that good. Bastard.

She bit down on her lip and lifted her hips in rhythm with his fingers. If he intended to keep this up, she might as well go along with it. Not that she had much choice since her body had already begun to ache for more from him.

"Another orgasm is always good." He followed up with another bite to her inner thigh that created an arc of pleasure that zinged between her legs. "But—" He raised to a sitting position on the leather bench seat and after one last thrust of his hand, pulled free from her body. "I think we should stop here."

Nina blinked. *What?* Was he joking? Too stunned for words, she sat there unmoving and watched him straighten his suit and remove an old-fashioned handkerchief from his breast pocket.

"Guess these come in handy after all." He used the bright white cloth to clean them both before shoving it and her panties into his attaché.

Having suddenly transformed into the perfect gentleman, Gabe helped her sit up and rearrange her clothing back to normal. Or as normal as they got after a mind blowing orgasm in the back seat of a car.

As she fixed her hair and dug through her bag for lipstick, he retrieved the paperwork and pen from the floorboard where he'd hastily flung them when...

Heat crept up her neck as she fully realized how intent he'd been on pleasuring her. It was only now she really comprehended how incredible it made her feel to know that she had that kind of effect on him. His need had been palpable. Nearly tasteable. That couldn't be faked, right?

"Here." He handed over the pen. "You need to sign the paperwork and then we're going inside to get this done. The sooner we're married, the sooner I can get back to my mission."

"Mission?"

He looked up, his eyes darker than ever. "Yes, babe. The mission. Making you come so much you pass out. It's just become my number one priority."

CHAPTER TEN

Gabe stared down at the ring on his finger and smiled. He was fully aware of the potential shit storm that would likely rain down on him for sneaking Nina off to the Justice of the Peace and he didn't care. Once the idea of Nina in his house and his bed as his wife had entered his mind, all other bets were off. Nothing else mattered.

He now had the means and hopefully the time to draw out her submissive nature and he planned to take full advantage. Yes, they still had the matter of her missing memory to deal with and all that potentially entailed, but priorities had changed and his need to possess her had roared to front and center.

"What are we doing here? I thought we were going straight to the airport."

Gabe looked out the window to see that they'd pulled up to her small cottage behind her lakeside cafe. After their civil ceremony, his directions to the driver had been explicit as he amended their itinerary.

"You didn't actually think I could ignore your declaration about a massive toy collection and not need to see it, did you?"

Her mouth popped open making him raise his eyebrows and set his lips in a firm line to keep from laughing.

"You want to see it right now? Seriously?"

"Babe, I don't just want to see it. I want to use it. Hell, I even want to watch you use it. That's just not something a man like me can get out of my mind."

Nina shook her head at him and reached for the car door. He grabbed her hand and pulled her back into his arms. "Not so fast, Mrs. Michaels." He pressed a light kiss to her mouth. "I have to ask. Are you sure you're ready for this? For me?"

A slow smile spread across her beautiful face. "A little late to ask me that now, isn't it?" She held up her left hand. "You've already put the ring on it."

"I'm serious, Nina. The minute we step out of this car, I'll have expectations."

"That's kind of a cold way to say you want to fuck me silly, isn't it?"

Gabe felt a growl deep in his throat. Her continual need to keep this light made it difficult to get a straight answer. "There's absolutely nothing silly about what I plan to do to you as soon as we're alone, baby girl. You should get that through your head right now. Let's just call this me being a gentleman one last time." He reached forward and grabbed one of her nipples through the thin dress she wore with no damned bra underneath. A fact that taunted him through their entire 'wedding'.

With enough pressure applied for her to realize he meant business, her mouth formed the perfect little O and he imagined spreading that circle wider with his cock.

"Thank God you're not as innocent as a typical virgin because I'm going to ruin you, baby," he warned. "By the time we're done here, you're going to be a dirty little ex-virgin who begs for my cock."

Her short gasp at his words wrapped around his dick and squeezed. He had her and damn well knew it.

Although, he already knew now they were

never going to be done. Maybe if he hadn't taken the time to sample her pussy before the ceremony he'd still be able to think straight. As it was, he simply couldn't stop this runaway train. There were simply not enough good intentions in the world to stop him from claiming what belonged to him now. Tonight he'd settle for possessing her body, but soon it would be everything else.

Especially her heart.

She mistakenly thought she could guard it from him by hiding behind little quips and excuses. He couldn't wait to show her otherwise.

"Let's go. Show me what you've got, sweet wife of mine."

Wordlessly, Nina climbed from the car and walked up to her front door with him right behind her admiring the view the whole way. She had a sweet, curved ass that made a man want to take a bite out of it.

He bit back a groan. What were the odds he could make her first time as memorable as possible if he couldn't get his thoughts under control? Every step she took, every word she spoke, made him so hard he wanted to explode.

Nina made quick work of the lock and he barely got a hold of her before she sprinted through the door. "Hold on. Let's make this official shall we?" He scooped her into his arms and carried her over the threshold. Old-fashioned? Probably. Necessary? Fuck yes.

Although now that he had her completely in his arms he didn't want to put her down. Since he'd been to her place many times and it was approximately the size of his living room, he knew his way around. He carried her in the direction of the bedroom.

"For someone with a potty mouth and a need for total control, you sure seem to have a romantic streak as well," she said, the humor barely restrained in her voice.

"Control and a man who speaks whatever is on his mind doesn't preclude his desire to take care of you. That's equally, if not more important than everything else." He entered her small bedroom and swung her to her feet. "Where is it?"

"Safe inside the big wardrobe in the corner." She pointed in the opposite direction she walked as she disappeared into the bathroom. "Oh and the combo is 0968746 to unlock it," she yelled through the open doorway.

Unable to curb his curiosity any longer, he

crossed to the floor-to-ceiling cabinet and opened
it up.

Holy shit.

The safe, as she put it, was the size of a refriger-
ator. Surely, that wasn't all toys. He entered the
code and pulled the heavy door open. What he
found blew his mind. Her collection rivaled his in
sheer number, with a somewhat different kind of
variety than his playroom toys offered.

He pulled out one of the velvet-lined drawers
and examined the size, shape and sheer number of
vibrators he found there. Where he had tools
designed for a Dominant to give both pain and
pleasure as necessary, hers were all about her
pleasure.

Damn.

Moving on, he opened another to find an array
of butt plugs also available in every size from small
to large. Good God, he'd hit the mother lode with
this one. As an ass man, he deemed this drawer
would definitely be his favorite.

The final drawer however, contained items he
had not expected. Nestled among the black velvet
that lined the entire space were some implements
that he was very well versed in. First, he picked
up the white leather paddle. He smacked it across

his hand and smiled at the stiff unbending feel of it.

This one had yet to be broken in. Perfect.

The other item that caught his eye was the black chained nipple clamps with tightening screws. Apparently, she had picked up more interests from her visits at Purgatory than she had let on.

He gathered half a dozen items, including the paddle and clamps, and placed them on the edge of the bed just as Nina emerged from her bathroom that also housed her closet.

She'd changed from the more formal lace dress and strappy heels she'd worn to the courthouse to a casual light blue sundress with pink flowers, a slim fitting denim jacket and her favorite well-worn cowboy boots that rarely left her feet.

"I think you're a little overdressed."

"For what?" she asked.

He turned and pointed to the stash he'd laid out on her bed.

The pink blush that colored her neck and face made him smile. They were her toys so it made no sense they would embarrass her now.

"I thought we were in a hurry to get to the airport?"

"I already told you, I've been derailed. Even more so now that I've seen what you've been hiding."

"I wasn't hiding anything. I've just kept it private. There's a difference. I highly doubt anyone would want to know the nitty gritty of my weird sex life anyway."

"I do. Babe, I've been waiting a long damn time for this. I want to know everything."

She looked down at the floor and moved her right boot in a circular pattern. "I would think that my collection speaks for itself. I mean, I guess you could say I have a toy fetish at this point."

Her attempt to poke fun at her needs sparked something inside him, reminding him that he had a mission for coming here. While he really did want to see her toy collection, he decided her first time deserved more, specifically somewhere she felt safe and completely at ease.

"Take off your clothes, Nina."

Her head jerked up and her gaze locked onto his.

He could read the momentary indecision as she warred over how she wanted to respond.

"Right now? Just like that?" she asked.

"You should probably get used to that, sassy

girl. I tend to take what I want, when I want it. Do we need to debate that point right now or are you going to do as I asked?"

She shook her head and sucked her bottom lip between her teeth.

"Good, then strip. I'll wait." He leaned against the wall, watching Nina toy with the bottom edge of her dress. She was obviously dying to follow his command, but he suspected she still needed to get her head out of the way. So he continued to wait.

His patience was rewarded.

She reached for the jacket and yanked it from her arms. Followed by the dress that she pulled over her head and tossed somewhere in the room. He couldn't see where because she'd just revealed what she wore underneath and he was pretty sure he'd just swallowed his tongue.

Hot fucking pink.

Underneath that sweet little sundress ensemble, Nina had hidden sexy as hell lingerie that basically hid nothing. Her taut nipples peeked out from behind the lace and beckoned him to come closer.

He did. In two strides.

"Damn, Angel. That's quite a surprise." He reached up and thumbed her nipples through the thin fabric and was rewarded again with a low moan. "You don't make it easy for a man to keep his wits about him."

"Do you need wits to have sex with your bride?" she asked.

Now it was his turn to moan. "I just need you naked and wet, baby."

With a surprisingly saucy grin, she reached behind her and unhooked her bra. A moment later, the garment was gone and her tits free. Unable to wait for her full compliance, Gabe cupped them. The way they filled his hands fit him perfectly. But it was the fact her eyes began to roll back that made his cock strain for freedom.

Knowing full well this wasn't going to last as long as he'd like, Gabe released her breasts and reached for the tiny scrap of lace some might call panties. He called them nothing but in the way.

When she stepped out of them, he realized she still had her cowboy boots on. He hesitated for a moment and then shrugged. Fuck it.

As it turned out, he only had so much patience for this process. How many days and nights had he spent planning this very moment down to the most meticulous detail? Although admittedly it had never gone quite like this in his head.

Learning of her virgin status had changed everything.

Now his whole body vibrated with the urge to get inside her as quickly as possible. His typical possessive streak had grown exponentially after she'd hesitantly agreed to his marriage proposal and he now had the most dire urge to make it official in every possible way.

First things first. Gabe reached around the back of her head and pulled her into a devouring kiss. His wife had a body made for sin that wouldn't quit. He had no idea what he'd done to finally deserve this because he probably didn't, but that didn't mean he wasn't going to take what she offered. No one had that kind of control, least of all him.

With their tongues tangling and heat building between them, Gabe slid one hand between her legs.

His head nearly exploded. She was so god damned wet he couldn't think straight. He only knew that once he got inside her everything would change. Logic and reason meant nothing when the woman you've waited forever for offers the sweet heat of her tight, little pussy.

"I'm ready," Nina whispered, her warm breath feathering across his skin. "Tell me what to do."

"Open my pants and take out my cock," he commanded before considering the consequences of her first touch.

She didn't hesitate as she unzipped his pants and freed him from the miserable confinement of his new suit. However, the instant sizzle of her skin against his aching erection ignited the simmer he'd tried to ignore that could only be handled one way.

Gabe lifted Nina, sliding her body against him until he nudged at her opening. "Wrap your legs around my waist."

She complied and he turned them until her back was against the wall and his dick was straining for freedom of a different kind.

He flexed forward an inch into her tight heat and paused, watching her reaction. Her eyes were closed and she was holding her breath.

"Look at me," he commanded, knowing full well she'd understand he wasn't making a request.

Her heat filled eyes opened and he eased forward a little more. Slow. Slow. Slow, being gentle as possible until he was fully seated inside her.

He sucked in air for a few deep breaths and

grappled with his control. It was so important for him to make her first time good. "Fuck, this is perfect. *You* are so fucking perfect. Hot, tight and all mine," he growled the last, not caring how animalistic he sounded. There was something about Nina that brought out his most primal possessive instincts beyond anything he'd encountered before or since her.

"Gabe," Nina said on a breathless moan.

"Yes, babe?" he asked, peppering her neck with alternating kisses and nips with his teeth.

"Why aren't you moving?"

He smiled. "Getting impatient, sweet girl?" He captured her lips before she could answer and devoured her with a deep kiss. With her legs wrapped around his waist and his hands cupping her ass, he could no longer wait.

He pulled back and thrust forward again, pressing Nina hard against the wall. Her resulting gasp made him smile and the word happy finally popped into his mind.

After years of waiting for her to be ready for a man like him, he'd managed to marry and fuck her in one day. His chest tightened again like it did every time he thought of her as his wife. Before today, he hadn't even dared to consider getting married. His single-minded focus had been on his need for a submissive. And whether or not Nina would become his.

His body always went haywire around her. His heart would speed up, his skin tingled and all the blood in his body always went south.

Now she was his.

All these thoughts were now jumbled in his brain as her wet heat strangled him. He pushed forward and ground against her clit, reminding them both who was in charge.

Her resulting moan slid down his spine. His hold on his control would soon be gone. As if to reinforce his need to display dominance, he slanted his mouth over hers and pushed her open with his tongue.

The fact she opened willingly and followed his lead made the Dominant preen. So excited by her responses, he imagined taking the next step and placing a collar around her neck that would tie them even closer than a wedding band did.

Soon. But first, he had to survive tonight.

"Fuck, you're so tight." He eased back a little and then pressed forward once again. Small digs that would deliver maximum friction for her pleasure.

Her gasp of ecstasy and the sharp point of her nails digging into his shoulders were making him lose control.

"Please, Gabe. I want more."

Her soft request broke something free inside him. He paused for only a second before he thrusted hard. There was nothing he could do now except pound into her like the obsessed man he was.

Years of denial needed to be erased from both their memories. Now he'd fuck her until she got so addicted to him the thought of leaving would never cross her mind again. No more walking away would be tolerated.

Gabe slammed into her body as her arms and hands tightened around him. There was nothing he could or wanted to do to stop this frenzied need.

"Oh shit, Gabe. I'm coming. I can't stop it!" She was screaming as she came and that very illicit sound unleashed his own orgasm as he dug in deep and poured what felt like his soul straight into her.

Uh oh.

A random token of reality slammed into him a little too late. With his dick buried as deep as it could go and her convulsing aftershocks milking him dry, he realized he'd forgotten a condom.

Fuck. What the hell had he been thinking? He hadn't been. That was the point. He was never in his right mind with Nina, especially since he'd gotten his first taste.

In the span of one day, he'd convinced her to marry him under suspect circumstances and now might have gotten her pregnant. None of which he felt an ounce of remorse for. How could he when it got him inside Nina after all these years?

Today, tomorrow or any other day of their life, he would do whatever it took to keep her as his. Nothing could stop him.

CHAPTER ELEVEN

*N*ina opened her eyes and then immediately shut them again against the bright Carolina sunshine blazing through her bedroom window. As she willed her eyes to adjust to the light, instinct kicked in and she shot up.

Oh shit. What time was it? She reached to scoop up her phone from the nightstand to check the time and found it not there.

What the hell?

When she began searching the room for the missing phone she got a whole lot more than she bargained for as the sight of half her toy collection at the foot of the bed brought the memory of the day and night before flooding back to her.

Everything came back. The good, the bad and the crazy.

She lifted her left hand to discover her marriage to Gabe had apparently not been a dream. Nina fell back against the pillows and breathed deep as she relived some of what they'd done the night before.

She'd had sex with Gabe—more than once. That fact alone pretty much blew her mind. The fact they were married though, that had to qualify as her most impulsive act to date.

She scrubbed her face with her hands and swallowed down her squeal of frustration. Of all the things she could have—

"Good, you're awake."

Nina shot to a sitting position to find Gabe emerging from her ensuite bathroom looking as fresh and gorgeous as always in yet another fine suit. Somehow, he seemed to have an endless supply of those lately.

"What have we done?" she groaned, ducking her chin.

A soft chuckle filled the room as Gabe moved closer to the bed. "Is that a rhetorical question or would you like me to recount the deliciousness of the last twelve hours? Or maybe you need me to show you."

"You're incorrigible. And crazy. How did I let you talk me into this?" she held up her hand and pointed to her brand new wedding ring.

"You weren't exactly coerced, babe. In fact, it was surprisingly easy to convince you what a good idea it was."

Nina kicked off the covers and climbed out of bed, ignoring the twinge of pain between her legs. She stood and crossed over to her bureau and dug through the drawers looking for something to wear. Whatever soreness she felt today had been well worth it. However, she needed to get dressed and get her head on straight before he whisked her off to the airport.

Coffee. She needed coffee.

"I have to go to the office for a while. There was a situation last night."

She stopped mid search. "Something at the club? What happened?"

He crossed to her and placed his hand on her bare hip, his fingers splayed wide. "Nothing I can't handle in a few hours. One of the club submissives broke serious protocol last night and it's my job to decide the appropriate punishment for her today."

Her head jerked up. "What? You're actually going to punish someone?"

His fingers tightened on her skin. "It's part of the job, Nina. Our clientele relies on me to keep crucial parts of Purgatory discreet. There are strict rules in place for all who volunteer to work the third floor. And when someone breaks a rule, it's my job to examine the infraction and decide how it should be dealt with. And whether or not a certain amount of damage control is needed."

"Does this happen a lot?"

He smiled down at her. "Not at all. Employees and guests alike treasure their time with us. It's rare anyone screws this up. Unfortunately, when it does happen it must be dealt with swiftly."

"I don't like the sound of this." It sounded barbaric at best and a little cloak and dagger at worst. Either way it made her uncomfortable.

"Trust me, Angel. In our world it's not that big of a deal."

And that was exactly the part that made her nervous. In *his* world. A place she still wasn't sure about. What if she never learned to like it? What would he do with her then? How could a man like Gabe want a wife who couldn't embrace his lifestyle?

"Babe, you're thinking too hard about this. I can see it. Stop. I only need a few hours at the office to straighten out a few details and then we can return to our plans. Tonight, we'll be on our honeymoon and I can show you first hand the heights of pleasure I want to give you."

A quick pulse in her lower body reminded her that despite the reservations swirling through her mind, the rest of her was one hundred percent on board with his plan.

He leaned forward and captured her lips. Immediately the heat inside her caught fire as he delved deep. By the time he pulled away, her focus had returned to the sensations he'd brought to life last night. He was right. She did want to explore that. If she didn't try then she'd never know.

"Why don't you go and visit Savannah today? I know how badly you wanted to talk to her yesterday and making that attempt before we leave could clear the decks one way or another. Either she talks to you and helps clear up some of your questions, or she refuses and then we take our next steps to getting at your memories."

"I thought you weren't going to let me go alone?"

He shrugged, cupping her chin with his free

hand. "I hope you can appreciate how difficult it is to let you go. But, as you've pointed out on many occasions, my wife, and I quote, you're a big girl perfectly capable of handling your own affairs. So you go, but promise me one thing."

"What's that?" she asked, suddenly feeling suspicious. This seemed way out of character for the Gabe she knew. He had to be hiding something about the situation at the club.

"Take my car and driver. I need to know you have back up. Just in case."

She rolled her eyes. "Anyone ever tell you that you're paranoid?"

He leaned into her again, this time pressing his full body against her naked one. The friction from the fabric of his suit and the weight of his body behind it teased her nipples and made them pebble instantly.

"I prefer cautious," he rumbled, his fingers digging into her hip again. When he pulled back, she looked down and confirmed he was as affected as she was.

She squeezed her eyes shut and willed herself not to jump him where he stood. The man was hella sexy and dangerous to her libido.

"If I didn't know how sore you have to be right now, I'd have you bent over that bed so I could pound into you, baby girl. I can't wait to feel your pussy squeezing me again."

Nina groaned. His filthy words had a way of making her willing to do anything to make them come true.

"Makes you wet just thinking about it doesn't it?"

She nodded, unsure if she could actually string a sentence together.

"Good. Think about me today and when we meet back here, I'm going to see how well your ass takes a plug. It's time to start your training."

Nina's legs wobbled, forcing her to reach out and grab his forearms to steady herself.

"Training?" she asked.

"Mmhmm." He cupped a breast and quickly tweaked a nipple until a slight burn bloomed inside her. "In addition to getting your ass ready for my cock, I'd like to experiment with a few other things. I'd like to see how you respond."

"What other things?" she asked, her voice a barely there whisper as the pain at her breast bloomed into voracious heat low in her body. Just the suggestion of him using one of her toys on her had her body and mind reeling with possibilities.

"One step at a time, baby girl. I've given you enough to keep your mind on me while you're gone, so let's not push it. Now go take a warm bath and give your body a rest before you run off to fight the world. Can you do that for me?"

She nodded. A bath sounded divine. And a good time to use one of her vibrators to maybe take the edge off. Her new husband had a way of keeping her on the ledge and making her needy.

The word husband still sounded so foreign. After years of friendship and some intense flirting on occasion, it wasn't easy to make this sudden leap to the next level. The level where he commanded her at every turn and in return gave her orgasm after orgasm. Speaking of...

"Oh lordy, I can see that mind of yours working overtime again. Look at me."

He tightened his fingers on her nipples, bringing her thoughts back into sharp focus. On a gasp, she looked up at him with the request for release on the tip of her tongue.

"I know what you need." He paused, his nose flaring. "Trust me, I do. And if I didn't need to leave ten minutes ago, I'd place you on your knees on that bed and give it to you."

He suddenly released her nipples and the rush of blood flow brought on another wave of sensual pain to wash over her.

"One other thing, Nina."

She looked up at him, the unspoken question between them.

"If you want to touch yourself today, that's fine, but no orgasm without me. Is that understood?"

Her eyes widened as his meaning sank in. This made her frown. "That's just mean," she said.

He chuckled. "Not mean, Angel. A little hard maybe, considering how much you ache right now, but never mean." He laughed again. "Okay, maybe a little mean. But trust me, I'm right there with you. You've made me hard as fucking hell and I can't wait to do something about it. So imagine the anticipation of waiting until we are together again and how hard I can make you come. I need to see that. Hell, I need to taste it flowing across my tongue."

He shook his head as if trying to clear that image from his head. That would be impossible, she knew. Because it was in her head too and she was pretty sure burned there forever. However, the idea he suffered alongside her made her stomach flutter.

"I'll wait for you. I promise."

"Mmmm." He reached up and grasped her face, running his thumbs across her lips. "That might be the sweetest promise anyone's ever made to me."

He bent down and kissed her. Gentle at first, until she opened her mouth and he slipped inside. The force of his kiss took her aback. Hunger between them arced as he deepened the kiss. Something she eagerly accepted without struggle. There would never be enough kisses in the world for her to not want this again and again.

When the kiss ended, she immediately felt the loss. He was pulling away from her to leave and she wasn't ready.

"Go take that bath, Nina. Think of me. Then tonight I will make sure your wait was worthwhile."

With that, he crossed the room and disappeared through the door. A moment later, the front door opened and closed. The loss of his intense proximity immediately cooled the room, reminding her that she stood there without a stitch of clothing on. She shook her head. How did he do that?

She sighed. Now she had to face the rest of her day all revved up on his dirty talk. And she doubted that orgasm-less bath was going to help one bit. Still. He'd been right that her body ached in more ways than one and she had a specialty bath bomb from her favorite store that would fix her right up. Soreness or not, nothing would keep her from the orgasmic bliss that her husband had promised her.

he drive to the county jail went by fairly quick this time of day with little traffic to impede their progress. However, with each passing mile, a knot in her stomach had started to form and it was still growing at a scary rate as she waited to be escorted to the room where visitors could talk to prisoners.

As instructed, Gabe's driver had been waiting for her in front of her house when she'd finally emerged. He'd ushered her into the back seat of a town car and proceeded to drive her downtown under an almost cloudless sky that did not match the nerves jumping in her stomach.

However, by the time they reached the building that housed the jail, a storm had rolled in and it was turning ugly. Even now, thunder cracked outside, further fraying her nerves.

Get it together, Nina.

While she remembered Savannah Lewis from her childhood when she visited Tucker, it had been many years since she'd seen her other than on the television during her recent arrest.

A guard called her name and motioned for her to follow. As they made their way down a long corridor, she wondered what she would find when they sat down. As the guard led her into a room filled with booths that were separated from the other side of the room by glass she figured whatever it was, she was about to find out.

"Booth number seven. Take a seat and the prisoner will come to you. Unfortunately, you only have ten minutes. Ms. Lewis has a treatment scheduled."

Nina wanted to ask what kind of treatment, but figured she'd better not waste any time if her clock was already ticking. She hurried to the booth and took her seat. A moment later, a loud buzzer sounded and Savannah Lewis walked through the door.

When she looked up and their gazes met, she stopped in her tracks. Something odd that Nina couldn't place crossed the woman's face. And a moment later, it was gone. Instead, the regal look she always associated with Tucker's mother settled in as she stood up straighter and removed any tell-tale signs of emotion from her face.

She sat in a chair directly across from her and Nina snatched up the phone handset that would allow them to talk. Savannah on the other hand did not move quickly. She stared at Nina blankly for several beats before finally reaching for the handset.

"Why are you here?" she asked, beating Nina to the punch.

Nina swallowed. Despite the awkward circumstances, there were questions she had to ask. So she pressed on. "We need to talk."

Mrs. Lewis shook her head. "No, we don't. I was very clear the last time we spoke. Did you not understand me when I said I never wanted to see or hear from you again? This is too dangerous."

This nugget of information hit Nina like a punch to the gut. "I don't recall that conversation at all. If you'd be so kind as to refresh my memory I'd really appreciate it." Suddenly, she felt like a small child again being lectured for showing up to see Tucker unannounced. How many times had this woman made it clear she didn't want her around and yet, here she was again hoping against hope that the other woman would shed some light on her missing memories.

"Don't patronize me, Nina. You know perfectly well I meant what I said. We agreed never to talk again and yet, here you are. Showing up out of the blue. For what? Are you trying to cause trouble?"

She shook her head. "I don't think so. But you don't understand. I—I can't remember the last time I saw you. The night of the—"

"Don't you dare say it." Savannah's face twisted in anger. "You made a promise and I damned well expect you to keep it."

Nina sighed. This wasn't going very well and she knew they were quickly running out of time. She'd have to get Mrs. Lewis back on track if she had a chance in hell of learning anything today. "You aren't hearing what I am trying to say and it's important. I don't remember. I mean REALLY don't remember. Whatever happened my brain has decided to block it from me. That's why I'm here. I need you to tell me what happened that night. Specifically, what I did that night. Please."

Savannah stared at her quietly. Her ability to keep her emotions hidden scared Nina a little.

What had happened in her life that made her learn such a skill? After a few more long seconds she couldn't stand it, she had to say something.

"Is this thing working? Did you hear me?"

Savannah nodded. "I heard you just fine. I'm just processing this new information. Are you really telling me that you have some sort of amnesia and truly can't remember what happened that night?"

"Yes and it's driving me crazy. I need to know. I don't care how bad it was. Anything is better than not knowing."

The other woman chuckled and the sound scraped down Nina's spine worse than nails on a chalkboard.

"You should always be careful what you wish for, darling. It just might come true."

Nina rolled her eyes. She didn't have time for this. Their time had to be half over by now. "Fine. Whatever. Just tell me. I really don't care. I just have to know."

Savannah's eyes narrowed and she compressed her lips, giving Nina her first real glimpse at the true age of the other woman. With the makeup and such that she still managed to wear while in jail, she looked completely put together despite the silly white jumpsuit they made her wear. (So much for the idea that all prisoners had to wear orange. Clearly that was a TV thing.) But with her mouth twisted and her eyes squinting, the well-worn wrinkles of age were clearly visible.

Tucker's mother no longer had the benefit of her youth to guard her. She tried to remember her age, but the information escaped her. Savannah had always been so perfectly coiffed that no one even bothered to question something so silly as her true age.

"If this is serious, then it's better you not know the details."

Her words brought Nina out of her head and back into the prisoner visitor room where the lights glared and the stark sparseness of it all began to match the void Nina felt in her memory.

"What's better is irrelevant. It's more important that I know what happened. What I did that night."

A smile completely void of happiness crossed Savannah's face, making the unease inside Nina ratchet yet another notch higher.

"It's better this way. In fact, this works perfectly as far as I'm concerned. I've confessed. What else matters? Go home, Nina. Forget about me. Forget about all this. Let that night go. We'll all be happier for it."

"How can you say that? I'm clearly not happy or I wouldn't be here and how can you be happy sitting in a jail cell?"

The other woman continued to stare blankly at her as if she'd completely tuned out.

Anger surged through Nina as she stood and slammed her hand down on the table. "Don't do this. Please. I can't stand it. I have to know."

Savannah was looking down at the table, now intent on something other than the conversation they were having. Nina followed her gaze.

"You're married?" Savannah asked.

She looked at the shiny new wedding band on her finger. "Yes, but—"

"To who?"

Nina blew out a breath. This conversation was beyond frustrating. "Not that it matters right now, but Gabe Michaels and I were married yesterday."

Savannah's head jerked up and their gazes met. This time the void of emotion had been replaced with something that actually looked real. Fear? No, that couldn't be it. Regret? She couldn't tell. Reading others' emotions had never been her forte.

"That's unfortunate," Savannah replied, the

sadness in her voice echoing what Nina saw in her eyes.

"What's that supposed to mean? Why would my marriage to Gabe, someone your son has embraced as almost a brother, be unfortunate?"

"Has he told you about his parents yet?"

The question out of the blue about Gabe's parents threw her off. Why in the world would that matter? "Of course I know what happened to his parents. Their tragic car accident has never been a secret."

Savannah shook her head. "Not his adopted parents. His real parents."

Nina stopped short. "Gabe's adopted?"

The sigh she heard through the handset did not bode well and Nina had a feeling whatever she was about to say next was going to be really bad.

"Yes, Nina, he was adopted. The lovely couple that raised him had nothing to do with his unfortunate birth."

"Unfortunate?!" Now she was getting pissed. How dare she? What right did she have—?

"Nina, dear, don't be so naive. You're better than that. Plus, you've been around this family since the beginning. Did you really never wonder why Mason took such an interest in a total stranger?"

"They went to college together. They played on the same football team. They were friends." All words she'd heard directly from Gabe.

Savannah shook her head again. "This is sad. I knew Mason keeping this a secret would come back one day and bite someone in the ass and it appears I was right. It looks like you're the one getting bitten, unfortunately."

None of the words coming out of Savannah's mouth made any sense to her. Why were they talking about Gabe and his parents instead of her father and the night he died? Who cared why Mason and her brothers took Gabe in, they--

A seed of something niggled at the back of her brain. Something horrific. "No, you are not saying that he--" She couldn't even say the words out loud.

"Wow. That took you long enough, my dear. Although I don't know why. You've been around Mason Sinclair your whole life. Have you ever seen him be so generous and accommodating to anyone other than family? Come on. Use that brain of yours. You are more than just a pretty face and a young body. They are--"

"Time's up," the guard behind Savannah yelled

as she stepped forward, interrupting the conversation at the worst possible moment.

"No!" Nina slapped the glass partition between them. "I need more time. They are what?" she screamed at Savannah.

"Sorry, ma'am." The guard turned to Savannah. "Put the handset down and let's go."

Mrs. Lewis hesitated briefly before standing and then she put the phone back to her head. "Go and see your mother. Ask her about your father. There is more to the story. It's not what you think—"

The guard grabbed the handset away from Savannah, slammed it down on its cradle and ordered her away from the table.

"No. Please. Don't do this. I need to know. What the hell is happening?"

She watched her say something to the guard, hoping it would have an effect.

But it was too late. Mrs. Lewis was forcefully dragged from the room screaming something back at her that Nina could not hear.

She watched in horror while sucking in gulps of air that didn't appear to be delivering oxygen to her brain as the room was now spinning.

Adopted.

Not what you think.

Mason.

None of the words going through her head could be strung together to make any sense. Because the bombshell that Savannah just dropped could not be true. No way. Now how never in a million years.

Except.

Mason. She was right about him. He kept a viciously tight circle, never letting anyone in except family. The only people who ever got through were Gabe and Rebecca and she might as well be part of the family at this point.

Family.

Sharp pain stabbed through her chest as she collapsed down into the chair. She fumbled for her phone stuffed in her pocket, but her hands shook so hard they wouldn't function right. When she finally got it free she stared down at the screen trying to remember who she'd been about to call.

"You can't use that in here. You'll have to go outside to make a call." The guard monitoring this side of the room came up behind her.

Although she heard the words, they didn't fully register. They sounded like they were coming through an underwater filter or something. Instead,

Savannah's words still jack hammered through her head loud and clear.

Her vision blurred as her brain allowed only one clear word to penetrate.

Brother.

"Are you all right?" The guard stepped closer.

She tried to nod, but moaned instead when the nausea of the truth hit her hard.

It couldn't be true. It just couldn't.

"You look a little pale. I think you should go. Maybe get some fresh air. I don't need no one passing out in here. I'm not into extra paperwork today."

Nina looked up at the guard frowning down at her and tried to stand. Yes, air. She needed way more.

Unfortunately, the lack of air in this tiny room made her head spin. Her stomach churned as she stood and before she could stop, she pitched forward and all the pain of Savannah's words vomited from her mouth as the entire contents of her stomach spewed onto the unhappy guard.

Not that it mattered. Her entire future had come crashing down on her. Suffocating her. In fact, now would be a good time to die.

Gabe Michaels was her half-brother.

CHAPTER THIRTEEN

$\mathcal{N}$ina climbed into the car after stumbling from the county jail and mumbled for the driver to take her to Purgatory. She had no idea how she was going to face Gabe with this information. Did he already know? That didn't seem possible. He would never do something like this to her.

Right?

RIGHT?!

The mere thought made her stomach churn, threatening dry heaves again. As if the information from Savannah had not been horrifying enough, throwing up on the female guard had taken the cake. Not to mention the woman had gone insane cussing her up one side and down the other before finally escorting her out of the building.

Now she sat in the back of the car feeling utterly and completely lost. Gabe. He was her rock and the one person she always turned to when her life turned to shit. And she'd married him!

Nina shut down her thoughts on that track. If she let her mind wander through the implications of that she was going to end up in the ER for a mental health consult. Her hold on her sanity felt that tenuous at the moment.

Fortunately or unfortunately as the case happened to be, the ride to Purgatory took no time at all. The driver pulled to the curb and stopped in front of the entrance.

"I'll wait here for you."

She shook her head and met the driver's gaze. "You don't have to. I can make my way from here."

"No, ma'am. I'll wait. Those are my instructions from Mr. Michaels."

Her stomach flipped at the sound of his name being spoken out loud. She didn't bother to argue with the driver as she opened the car door and stepped out.

She looked up at the nearly unmarked building except for the emblazoned P logo on the heavy wooden double-doored entrance. She couldn't go around back and use the employee entrance because she didn't have a key card for that. Which made sense considering she'd never needed to come here during off hours before. That left her only option to knock and hope someone heard her.

Unwilling to talk to anyone she knew on the phone, she'd not bothered to call ahead to let anyone know she was coming. Part of her wanted to climb right back into the car and have the driver take her anywhere but here.

Maybe she should have gone to Mason first. There had to be some sort of explanation about this mess. Except if what Savannah had said were true then it was her oldest brother who was largely responsible for this insane travesty. If that ended up the case, she'd deal with Mr. Pain In Her Fucking Ass later.

Right now, she did what she always did in times of total disaster. She ran to Gabe. Her hand stilled in mid air. Would this be the end of all that? Had her biggest fear come to fruition? Not only would she lose a man she thought might hold her future in his hands, but she'd lose her best friend too.

Her stomach threatened mutiny once again. God, how much more of this could she take?

"Nina? What are you doing here?"

She froze at the sound of Tori's voice on the sidewalk behind her. What the hell, God? Could he seriously not cut her a break?

Her life had imploded in a matter of minutes and now she had to pretend everything was fine? Screw it. Tori had already witnessed her at her worst that drunken day in her office. So what the hell? What did a little more matter in the grand scheme of her ridiculous life?

She slowly turned to her friend, knowing full well there was no way out of it. "Tori. What are you doing here? Aren't you supposed to be at the cafe?" It was the middle of the day and there would be customers waiting.

"I could ask you the same thing. I mean the being here part. I had to come. I was summoned by Gabe about an incident. But don't worry Levi's holding down the fort for us until I can get back."

Oh shit. The incident.

Whatever the hell that meant. She'd forgotten all about her discussion with Gabe this morning about some employee breaking the rules.

"You're the one who broke some sort of rule last

night?" She didn't want to think about Gabe having to punish her friend.

She shook her head. "Oh no. Not me. I know better than that, believe me. But Levi and I were here last night and I overhead what happened. So he asked me to come in."

"Well, I guess you can let me in then. I was about to pound on the door in the hopes someone heard me."

Tori laughed, a hesitant sound that made it clear her friend wasn't buying whatever she was trying to sell.

"Is everything okay? You seem, I don't know--off."

Nina straightened her spine and plastered a smile on her face that she hoped her friend believed. "I will be. I just need to talk to Gabe."

Tori hesitated as if she wanted to say more. Instead, she pulled a keycard out of her pocket and handed it to Nina. "Here, I won't need this anymore today so you can go ahead and go on in. Gabe's in his office, but I--uh--would wait until he's done with his meeting. Things are not going well.

For once in her life, Nina's curiosity didn't even bother to stand up and notice. She didn't give one fuck about Gabe's other problems right now. She could guarandamntee they weren't as important as what she had to say.

"Thanks." She took the offered card and started to walk away when an idea occurred to her. "Hey, Tori. I'm going to be going out of town for a couple of days. Do you mind taking care of the cafe for a few more days? I know it's asking a lot at this point, but I'll be back to work real soon I promise." She highly doubted that, but she didn't need to tell anyone else that just yet.

"Sure, it's no problem. You know I love working in your kitchen. It's a blast."

Nina sagged in relief. She didn't want to close the doors quite yet, but no way could she deal with being around here much longer when everyone learned the truth.

With that, she waved and slipped around the building to the employee entrance.

———

The third floor that housed the private play areas and the owner offices felt eerily quiet in the middle of the day. She never came up here. For one, she wasn't officially a member and they had strict rules about that kind of thing and secondly, she didn't want to.

She'd always feared coming up here would mean she'd have to watch Gabe play with other women. A sight she never wanted to see. A fresh bout of nausea poured through her and she clutched her stomach.

She approached Gabe's office with what felt like lead feet forcing her to use extra effort to make it to the end of the hall. Unfortunately, Liz, Gabe's secretary, was sitting guard outside his office. Well, not so much guard as just sitting at her desk, but it felt like she might be standing guard ready to stop anyone from going in.

Yes, paranoia had definitely set in.

Nina slapped on another fake grin and greeted the secretary she'd met once or twice at a Christmas party or something. She couldn't quite recall. "Hi, Liz."

The woman looked up, shock crossing her face at Nina's sudden appearance.

"Uhm. Hi, Nina. Can I—uhm—help you with something?"

"Nah, just here to see Gabe." She avoided meeting the woman's gaze any further and headed towards Gabe's closed door.

"Unfortunately, he's in a meeting right now and can't be disturbed. He might be a while, too. But if you want to leave him a message, I can make sure he gets it as soon as he's free."

Shit.

She contemplated how to handle this. It had taken everything she had left to give just to get this far. The idea of sitting here for what could be a very long time seemed intolerable.

"I'm afraid what I need to tell him can't wait." She hurried to the door before the secretary could stop her. The woman yelled for her to stop, but she was too late.

Nina burst through the door and came up short. If she'd thought things went bad at her visit to the jailhouse, that seemed almost minor in comparison to what she walked into in Gabe's office. And Savannah's bombshell had been so far from minor it wasn't even in the same ballpark.

"What the fuck?" Nina glared.

There were two men flanking Gabe's desk and kneeling between them with her back to the door was a naked woman with her arms raised and attached to Gabe's desk with a pair of black leather cuffs.

In the middle of the room stood Gabe, his suit

jacket off, his sleeves unbuttoned and pushed up to his elbows and a big, heavy flogger resting in his right hand.

"Nina."

"I'm so sorry, Sir. I tried to stop her."

Nina's jaw ticked with anger as the secretary tried to explain herself. Finally, she interrupted, "It's true. She did tell me that you were in a meeting and couldn't be disturbed. I just took it upon myself to ignore her and come in anyway. Now I can see why you didn't want anyone to interrupt."

"Nina," Gabe said her name like a warning and that did nothing except fuel her anger that grew by the second.

"Don't." She held up her hand in an attempt to stop him. Not that she expected him to listen.

"It's not what you think."

She rolled her eyes at his clichéd statement. How many women in her role had heard that line before?

"You know what? I really don't care. It's fucked up, whatever it is."

She stepped forward, propelled by the sudden rush of adrenalin this little episode had given her. "What I do care about however, is simple. I have just one question for you and I need the truth. For once, someone had better tell me the truth."

"Nina, I can see something has you upset. But whatever it is I don't think this is the time or the place for it."

She ignored him. "DID. YOU. KNOW?"

"Did I know what?"

"Did you know that you were adopted?"

Confusion crossed his face for a moment before he answered. "Of course I did. My parents told me when I was a teenager. But what the hell does that have to do with anything? Why are you so angry?"

"Angry? You think I'm angry. I'm way beyond angry. How could you not tell me? I mean, what did I do to deserve all these lies from everyone in my life? Huh? Tell me!"

She'd gone past angry and straight to hysterical and illogical. She knew it and couldn't stop it. And now she was stuck having the most devastating conversation of her life over a naked woman chained to her husband's desk.

How could she have ever lived this life with him anyway? She'd never be able to accept this kind of thing that is normal to him, because it's NOT normal.

"Nina, you aren't making any sense. I didn't do anything to you, nor did I lie."

Before she could focus her next words, the door burst open again and slammed against the wall. They all turned to see Mason storm through the door and her stomach dropped. Somehow her need to talk to both Gabe and Mason was about to turn into a three-ring circus.

"What the fuck is the meaning of this?" He held up his hand where a stack of papers were clutched in it. The prenup she presumed. Apparently, Victor had delivered it already.

Mason charged forward. "How could you do this behind my back? You fucking made a promise to me not to pursue her."

Gabe sighed. "Goddamn it. Doesn't anyone respect a closed door around here?"

Nina slowly turned back to Gabe and glared at him. What the actual hell was happening?

"Fuck you, Gabe Michaels. Just fuck you. If you knew all along that you were adopted, then maybe you should have taken the time to find out who your real parents are. Because I'm pretty sure that if you knew that Reverend Lewis was your father, then you wouldn't have done something as sick as marry me. That would go so far beyond twisted. Even for a pervert like you."

Half the room gasped at the bomb she dropped. And of course just saying it out loud made her sick all over again. But she'd committed to it now. Might as well go for broke.

"That's right," she held up her ring finger for all to see. "He married his sister. Fucking hilarious, right?"

"What?!!!" Gabe roared, the sound nearly vibrating her internal organs with its anger.

"Shut the fuck up, Nina. You don't know what you're talking about," Mason seethed from behind her. "Just shut the fuck up already. We will discuss this in private."

"I will not shut the fuck up, brother dearest," she yelled at Mason. "This is your fault too. You knew. You had to know!!"

Gabe turned on Mason. "Tell me she's wrong."

Mason for once in his life remained silent.

"Say something!" Gabe roared. "Tell her she's wrong. I would never do that to her. Tell her!"

"This is not the place."

"Fuck the place. TELL HER!"

Mason fished his hands through his hair and sighed. "Jesus Christ, Gabe. I can't just—"

"TELL ME THE TRUTH." Nina had had it. She was so sick of lies on top of lies and all the secrets... Her entire life was one big cruel lie. She couldn't take it anymore.

"Fine." Mason turned to her. "Reverend Lewis is Gabe's biological father. But—" he hesitated and she felt the upheaval coming on all over again. "I never wanted to have to tell you this. If not for this asshole forcing you to marry him, you could have lived without more shit in your life."

"Mason if you don't stop making excuses..."

"Nina, stop," Mason said. "I'm getting there. I just didn't want this to be how you found out."

"Found out what?" She and Gabe yelled together.

"Reverend Lewis is not *your* biological father."

Nina stood there shell shocked as real pain coursed through her. Apparently everyone in her life *had* lied to her. Gabe, her mother, her bro—

No. She choked back a sob. They weren't her brothers. And just like that, clarity consumed her as she spun around and headed for the door.

"Nina, stop. We need to talk about this." Gabe's deep, angry voice didn't even penetrate this time. She'd had enough.

"You can all go fuck yourselves." She grabbed

the door handle and pulled the heavy wood door closed behind her. Enough was enough.

———

Thank you so much for reading GABE'S OBSESSION!

I hope you love Gabe and Nina. Their story concludes in *Gabe's Reckoning*, available now.

A lie. It's all been a lie. Now she has to run.

Screw that. Gabe has staked his claim and hell if he's going to let that go. **She. Is. His**. She can run, but she sure can't hide. If she's gone, then so is he. Purgatory can go to...well, hell.

Nina should have read the prenup they signed a little closer. He made it clear he didn't want her money, but he also made it crystal that she belonged to him in ways she hasn't even thought of yet.

And who their parents are doesn't change one damned thing. Neither does murder. If she's got blood on her hands he DOES NOT care.

But the lies DO have to stop. One way or another this family has to come clean. Even if it costs them everything.

One-click GABE'S RECKONING now!

And sign up for my newsletter to find out about new books... www.emgayle.com/newsletter

If you loved Gabe's Obsession, you'll love the sensual and exciting New York Times Bestselling Pleasure Playground series.

The first book PLAY WITH ME is available to one-click now!

And if you haven't read the Purgatory Club series that started it all, the first novella ROPED is FREE to one-click!

Katie has a desire for rope and she's had her eye on riggers Leo and Quinn for quite some time. Week after week she goes to the club and watches them tie up women from afar, while she imagines their rough rope against her own skin.

Now the two hunky men have decided to make their move. But is plus-sized Katie ready to turn her fantasies into reality?

Sign up for my **newsletter** to find out when I have new books!

You can also join my Facebook group, **EM Gayle Reader Group**, for exclusive giveaways and sneak peeks of future books.

I appreciate your help in spreading the word, including telling a friend. Reviews help readers find books! Please leave a review on your favorite book site.

Turn the page for an excerpt from GABE'S RECKONING...

EXCERPT FROM GABE'S RECKONING

Gabe Michaels stared at the door to his office that Nina, his new wife for all of a whopping twenty-two hours, had just slammed out of after telling them all to go fuck themselves.

Part of him wanted to charge after her and make her listen to what he had to say. And part of him still couldn't comprehend what had just happened.

As much as they needed to talk right now, there was someone else he had to deal with first. Shutting down the emotions for the woman he'd impulsively married after learning she was saving herself for a committed relationship, he turned and faced the room of shell-shocked witnesses.

Mason, his boss, mentor, and supposed friend reacted first. "Well, that didn't go well."

Gabe's eyes narrowed at the man he thought he knew. "Shut the hell up. This is your fault."

Mason's face darkened. "My fault? Fuck you, Michaels. If you hadn't broken your promise this never would have happened. I never wanted her to know all this shit and I especially didn't want her to ever find out like this."

Gabe shook his head before turning to the rest of the occupants in the room. He'd deal with Mason in private.

As if on cue, his secretary picked up on his unspoken wishes as soon as their gazes met. She turned to the two Doms still standing by his desk who had at some point released their submissive from her shackles and covered her in one of his many care blankets he kept in a basket near his desk.

"Gentlemen, I think that's our cue to take our leave. If you'd like, I can escort you to one of the other private rooms for your use."

Leo, one of the regular Purgatory riggers turned to Gabe. "Are we done here then?"

Gabe nodded. The previous all-important issue of their submissive Katie breaking discretionary protocol no longer seemed so dire. Not with Nina gone to God knows where and the emotional bombshell of both of their parentage still ricocheting through his mind.

It had taken less than sixty seconds to flip his world upside down.

"What exactly was going on here anyway?" Mason asked.

Gabe stared at him unseeing anything other than a man who had lied to him over and over for years. The betrayal of a long friendship that threatened to choke him now. And he wasn't about to accept him omitting the truth wasn't technically a lie. A lie was a god damn lie and as lies go, this one had been a doozy.

Finally, he shrugged. "Private issue. It's over now."

The submissive between the two Doms whimpered. Probably grateful for the interruption that saved her from further punishment. Although if he knew Leo and Quinn, and he did, they were far from done. He had no doubt that Katie would not break club protocol again.

And if he hadn't been an arrogant jackass, he could have avoided this scene altogether and never allowed Nina to visit Savannah alone. There were so many things he could have done differently to change the clusterfuck of today.

Mason's eyes narrowed and Gabe half hoped the man might push for more. Let him push. He'd end up with a hell of a lot more than he bargained for. It didn't matter that Mason stood a couple of inches taller than him, or that he had a mean streak that made for a formidable opponent.

They'd trained together more than once and Gabe already knew he could hold his own. Add in the rage whipping through his blood and he had no doubt he'd best the fucker.

When the door finally closed behind the last of his other guests, Gabe turned his attention solely to Mason.

"That is really what you wanted? For Nina to never know the truth? You really are an asshole, you know that? Did it never dawn on you that knowing that bastard Reverend wasn't her biological father might have made her happier? She's lived in agony for more than a decade. Hell, probably longer than that believing all the lies you people have force fed her. What the fuck is wrong with you? Why is the truth such a difficult answer?"

"You should be careful what you say here. You

don't know shit about what I've had to do to protect this family. And now that the cards are out on the table you should know that includes you. In fact, I've done everything in my power to protect her and every other defacto sibling I've uncovered. You think my job is easy? Just fuck you, man. You don't understand shit."

"Right now I don't care about me and I certainly don't care about what you've been through. It's all about her," his voice rose with every word. "She's been traumatized. How do you know the truth wouldn't have changed whatever it is she's got locked up in her head? Maybe had she known he was not her father, whatever happened that day wouldn't have happened and we all wouldn't be walking around on eggshells afraid this little house of cards you've built wasn't about to implode?"

The dark look Mason shot him would have likely cut down any other man. But he'd seen and done enough. He would no longer accept any more bullshit from this family.

"I didn't know he wasn't her father back then. Hell, I wasn't even sure I knew anything back then. It was all a damned guess until after he died and Victor came to me." Mason took another step closer, his face twisting with anger. "It's true I'm a bastard. I know this just as well as you do. Even Rebecca knows that and for some unknown reason, she still loves me. But—and this you'd better get through your thick skull right now—I do love my family. All of them, and that will always include Nina." He hesitated a moment before he continued, his face dark with his own rage. "Now don't get me wrong, I've never been the best when it comes to the whole love thing. I've screwed that up plenty of times. Yet, I still do everything in my power to hold us all together. That's what I do and it's what I will do until I die, no matter the cost."

Some of the anger deflated from Gabe. He didn't like it, but it was a relief to know that Mason couldn't have done anything to prevent their father's death and Nina's pain. But this family was falling apart at the seams and maybe, just maybe...

"Maybe you need to rethink your stance on the whole damned thing." Gabe fought at the nausea his thoughts were giving him. "Maybe this family is cursed. You ever think about that?"

"That's ridiculous. I don't believe in curses."

Gabe shook his head. "You don't have to take that literally. But, maybe this family doesn't need a puppet master anymore. You ever think of that? You say you've done nothing but fight to keep them together. Well, maybe they don't need or want to stay together anymore. Let it go, Mason. I'm starting to believe that together we're all toxic. I'm all for togetherness, but sadly that doesn't work in every case. Sometimes the best course of action is to go your separate ways."

Too angry to continue, he slammed out of his office and headed towards the building exit. He'd said all he had to say on this subject. What really mattered to him was finding his wife. There were more than a few things he needed to say to her and it was time to set the record straight and spank her ass red while he was at it.

Want to read more? Click here to download GABE'S RECKONING now!

WHAT ALEX WANTS

ALEX TAKES

Pleasure Playground Series:

PLAY WITH ME (also available in paperback & audio)

POWER PLAY (also available in paperback)

Single Title:

TAMING BEAUTY

BOOKS WRITING AS ELIZA GAYLE

Southern Shifters Series:
DIRTY SEXY FURRY
MATE NIGHT
ALPHA KNOWS BEST
BAD KITTY
BE WERE
SHIFTIN' DIRTY
NEVER KISS A WOLF
BEAR NAKED TRUTH
ALPHA BEAST

Devils Point Wolves:
WILD
WICKED

WANTED
FERAL
FIERCE
FURY

Pentacles of Magick Series:
UNTAMED MAGICK
MAGICK IGNITED
FORCE OF MAGICK
MAGICK PROVOKED

Single titles:
VAMPIRE AWAKENING
WITCH AND WERE
ALPHA WOLF RISING

Made in the USA
Las Vegas, NV
30 October 2022

58433774R00120